AF662730

DP SINHA

TWO CLASSICAL PLAYS FROM INDIA

DP SINHA

TWO CLASSICAL PLAYS FROM INDIA

Vitasta
LET KNOWLEDGE SPREAD

Published by
Renu Kaul Verma
Vitasta Publishing Pvt Ltd
2/15, Ansari Road, Daryaganj
New Delhi-110 002
info@vitastapublishing.com

ISBN 978-93-86473-26-4
© DP Sinha and Pratichi Mathur, 2018
MRP ₹425

All Rights Reserved.
No part of this publication may be reproduced, stored in a retrieval system, or transmitted in any form, or by any means—electronic, mechanical, photocopying, recording or otherwise—without the prior permission of the publisher. Opinions expressed in this book are the author's own. The publisher is in no way responsible for these.

Cover and layout by Vits Press
Printed by Vikas Computer and Printers

For my daughters
Prachi, Pratichi and Usha

CONTENTS

ONCE IN INDIA

The violence of non-violence

Translated from Hindi by
Ripa Ajmera

ONCE IN INDIA

The violence of non-violence

SYNOPSIS

Once in India is a historical play based on a historical event that took place about twenty-two centuries ago which constitutes the core of the play. But the play is not mere narration of history. It is a creative exploration of those times, in dramatic idiom, to give contemporary audiences a meaningful theatrical experience.

The history

Alexander the Great invaded India in 326 BCE. His invasion remained confined to the peripheral kingdoms on the northwestern borders of India. He had to abandon his ambition to conquer India because his men rebelled and refused to go any further. After Alexander's death, the Governors and Satraps in the conquered lands became independent. They divided the empire between themselves. Of these, Seleucus Nicator, with his capital in Mesopotamia, invaded India again, but was defeated by the Indian King Chandragupt Maurya in 305 BCE. As a result, Seleucus ceded some Afghan and Iranian territories and gave the Indian King a Greek princess in marriage.

After Seleucus' death, his Kingdom got fragmented into many smaller Greek kingdoms. One such kingdom emerged in Afghanistan, with its capital in Bactria (modern-day Balkh), whose rulers were called Indo-Greek rulers. Cut off from their homeland for over a century, many Greek Kings converted to Buddhism. Of these Indo-Greek Kings, Demetrius (205-170 BCE) and Minender (865-155 BCE) are the most well-known. They invaded India to complete Alexander the Great and Seleucus Nicator's unfinished agenda, which they did with some success.

King Brihadrath was on the throne of Magadh at the same time as King Minender was on the throne of Bactria. He was a descendent of King Chandragupt Maurya, who had foiled Seleucus' invasion and defeated him. Unlike Maurya, King Brihadrath was a pacifist. He converted to Buddhism and was a votary of non-violence. Frustrated by the King's diffidence and vacillation in taking on the Indo-Greek invaders, the Army Chief Pushyamitr Shung decided to depose the King. He invited the King to inspect the army. While the King was doing this, Pushyamitr beheaded him in full view of the soldiers, occupied the throne, and threw out the Indo-Greek invaders. The core of the play is based on this first—and last—recorded army coup in India's history of 5,000 years.

The play

A dimension of this play exists in the realm of ideas. We are conditioned to view life in contradictory dyads, such as good and bad, rich and poor, past and present, traditional and modern, materialistic and spiritual, violent and non-violent, etc. But there are no such sharp distinctions between black and white in reality; there are also shades of gray. By courageously embracing out-of-the-box thinking, the play points to a third dimension, which is nonaligned with traditionally opposite, binary elements.

The Truth is one, indivisible and inclusive; it aims for the peace and welfare of all of humanity. From this perspective, even a heinous act like murder, committed to further the peace and welfare of mankind becomes a spiritual act.

In ancient India, before the advent of Buddhism, Indians did not believe in the principle of absolute non-violence; they discriminated between violence against evil and violence against the noble. For ancient Indians, violence against the noble, innocent, and good was bad, while violence against evil was good and desirable. In this context, it may be noted that in the Sanskrit language there are two words for manslaughter: "*vadh*" and "*hatya*." If an evil man is killed for the safety, security, and welfare of society, it is called *vadh*. If a man is killed for personal vendetta or gain, it is considered *hatya*. While *hatya* is a sin and condemnable, *vadh* is praiseworthy and necessary. In the context of *Once In India*, the Army Chief Pushyamitr kills King Brihadrath, whose vacillating non-violent resistance would have otherwise led to the massacre of millions of Indians. In doing so Pushyamitr committed an act of *vadh*, not *hatya*. The play thus illustrates how, in certain circumstances, even the evil act of killing another man becomes ethical and socially desirable.

Non-violence has been an obsessive concern amongst Indians since the inception of Indian civilization. Indians believe in absolute non-violence; that is, non-violence even in the face of evil. They do not realize that non-violence is unable to resist evil forces, and that this, in effect, actually promotes evil and can ultimately lead to the annihilation of all that is noble. Lord Krishna had warned Indians against absolute non-violence in the classical Indian spiritual text *The Bhagavad Gita*. Krishna pronounced the limits of non-violence in unequivocal terms when he exhorted the warrior Arjun to take up arms against evil, for the purpose of upholding peace and righteousness. It may also be mentioned that all of the Hindu deities are always depicted with weapons in their arms, which are symbolic of their readiness to fight for righteousness. The Goddess Durga carries a trident and Goddess Kali is armed with a sword. Of the male deities, Shiva carries a trident, Vishnu has a discus and a club and Raam has a bow and arrow. But, the Hindu mind has refused to follow the example of its deities, as Indian history demonstrates throughout the centuries.

India succumbed to the Muslim invasion in 1192 CE because the Indian King hesitated and vacillated whether and how much to defend the country. He did not want to shed the invading soldiers' blood. The King's piety resulted in the entire country passing into tyrannical foreign rule for 600 years.

Absolute non-violence is a Hindu cultural frailty. Even the most noble and well-intentioned Mahatma Gandhi, the embodiment of non-violence, was not free from this frailty. When World War II broke out, Gandhi went to the British Viceroy, Lord Linlithgow and told him that the British should fight Adolf Hitler with absolute non-violence. He told Lord Linlithgow that the British should surrender their homes, their wealth and themselves to Germany, which would lead the British to ultimate victory over the Germans. Fortunately, the Viceroy did not abide by Gandhi's advice; otherwise, the whole world would have come under the Nazi sway.

GEOGRAPHY

Bactria: Present-day Balkh in northern Afghanistan; capital of the Indo-Greek Kings in the 2nd century BCE.

Gaandhaar: An ancient name for the modern-day city of Kandhar in Afghanistan.

Gangaa: A river in India revered as holy by Hindus.

Magadh: The name of an empire ruled by the Maurya Dynasty in the 2nd and 3rd centuries BCE, with its capital at Paataliputr.

Mysore: Name of a city in South India famous for jewelry-making.

Paataliputr: Capital of Magadh Empire; present-day Patna city in the state of Bihar, India.

GLOSSARY

Aaryaa: An honorific for women.

Alexander the Great: The Greek King who invaded India in 326 BCE. He could only conquer some peripheral territories on the northwest border of India because his army revolted.

Angulimaal: A bandit according to Buddhist legend whom the King's forces could not subdue. Lord Buddha approached him alone. Angulimaal surrendered to Buddha and became a Buddhist monk.

Arjun: A warrior who refused to fight for righteousness due to his compassion and concern for human life.

Arthashaastr: A book on statecraft written in 4th century BCE by Chanakya.

Ashokaaraam: The Buddhist monastery named after King Ashok in 3rd century BCE.

Bahujana Hitaay Bahujana Sukhaay: Lord Buddha's injunction to monks to "go spread Buddhism for the welfare and happiness of the majority of mankind."

Bhante: The term of address used for Buddhist monks.

Braahmans: The scholarly people who constituted a caste in India.

Buddha: The founder of the Buddhist religion in India in the 6th century BCE.

Buddham Sharanam Gacchaami: The most well-known Buddhist prayer, meaning *"I take refuge in Buddha."*

Buddhist: Name for a follower of Buddhism, a religion founded by Gautam Buddha.

Chakravartee: The term used for powerful kings in ancient India who subdued neighboring kings.

Cheever: An ancient Paalee word for maroon-colored Buddhist garments.

Dhamma: The Paalee equivalent of the Sanskrit word *Dharma.*

Dharma: The Sanskrit word for everything noble and positive, such as duty, good deeds, charity, altruism, ethical values, compassion, religion, etc.

Dharm-mahaamaatra: The name of a class of administrators created by King Ashok whose responsibility was to ensure that all citizens follow *dharma.*

Dhyaan: Meditation; attention.

Guru/Gurudev: The spiritual teacher.

Har Har Gange: A playful expression of reverence for the river Gangaa, which a devotee chants after taking his first dip in the river; literally meaning, *Hail Mother* Gangaa.

Kaling Conquest: The war waged by King Ashok against the Kaling Kingdom of India, in which more than 100,000 people were killed and an equal number were wounded and maimed. This conquest moved King Ashok so much that he decided never to wage war again.

Karma: Literally meaning *action* or *deed* in the Vaidic and Buddhist traditions. It is part of the belief system of all religions of Indian origin. All Indic religions believe that one's good or bad deeds (*karmas*) committed in this life determine the quality of one's next life.

Kautily: The author of *Arthashaastr*, a book written in 4th century BCE on polity and statecraft.

King Ashok: The King of the Maurya Empire in 3rd century BCE, known in history as the first pacifist King. He gave up war as part of State policy and devoted himself entirely to the welfare of humanity.

Krishna: Believed by Hindus to be a reincarnation of God in a human body, to protect the noble and destroy the evil. Also called "Lord Krishna."

Kumbh fair: A massive congregation of millions of Hindus held every twelve years since ancient times on the confluence of the rivers Gangaa and Yamuna.

Lotus feet: Traditionally, the feet of the divine or gurus are reverentially described this way.

Maar: The god of sex and desire in the Buddhist tradition.

Mahaabhaag: A form of address to a king in ancient times.

Mahaaraaj: Literally meaning "great king" in Hindi and Sanskrit; a form of address to a king in ancient times.

Maalaa: Term for a garland as well as a rosary.

Maurya: Name of the Empire and Dynasty that ruled in India in the 2nd and 3rd centuries BCE, with its capital in the city of Paataliputr.

Mauryan: One who belongs to Maurya clan.

Nirvaana: A Buddhist concept in which a soul, due to good *karma*, gets free of the cycle of birth, death, and rebirth and attains Ultimate Buddhahood.

Paalee: The language of the common people of ancient India from the 2nd to 6th centuries BCE.

Paarseeks: Name given to Persian people.

Pashtoons: Aggressive, war-like people living on the northwest frontiers of India (now in Pakistan).

Patanjali: The 2nd century BCE Yoga Guru and author of *The Yoga Sutra*, the seminal work on the system of Yoga.

Prajaamukh: People's representative in the Mauryan King's Court.

Prayaag: Name of a city where the Kumbh fair has been held since ancient times.

Raam: Believed by Hindus to be a reincarnation of God in a human body to protect the noble and destroy the evil. He is the hero of the Indian epic *Ramayan* who rescued his wife Seetaa and killed the demon Raavan who had abducted her.

Raavan: A villain in the epic *Ramayan* who abducted Raam's wife Seetaa and was ultimately killed by Raam.

Renunciate: An individual who withdraws from the world and devotes his or her entire life to the service of God and society.

Samaadhi: The ultimate stage attained by an individual in meditation.

Sangh: A Buddhist order.

Sanskrit: An Indian language of ancient origins.

Seetaa: Raam's wife.

Senaapati: The Sanskrit equivalent of "Commander-in-Chief."

Seleucus Nicator: One of the generals in Alexander the Great's army. After Alexander's invasion of India (in 326 BCE), Nicator invaded India in 305 BCE and was defeated by the Indian Maurya King Chandragupt.

Shaktipaat: In the Yoga context, the transmission of energy from a Guru to his or her disciple, wherein the Guru places his or her hand on top of the disciple's head.

Shramans: Term for non-Vaidic (usually Buddhist and Jain) monks.

Tathaagat: An appellation used for Gautam Buddha.

The Four Noble Truths: Propounded by Gautam Buddha in his first sermon—the first of which is that there is suffering in life.

Tripitaka: The Buddhist holy text—similar to the Bible in Christianity.

Ujjain: Name of an Indian city.

Vaidya: Means doctor in Sanskrit.

Vaidic: Followers of the ancient Hindu holy text called the *Vedas*; non-Buddhists.

Vishkanyaa: Literally meaning *poison girl*. In ancient India, a woman sent by one king to poison another.

Yoga: A spiritual system and practice leading to Samaadhi.

Yogah karmasu kaushalam: One of Patanjali's Yoga *Sutras* (aphorisms) in his seminal work *The Yoga Sutra*, meaning "Yoga is dexterity in action."

Zeus: The famous Greek God.

THE CHARACTERS

Minender	The Indo-Greek King, with his Capital in the city of Bactria (modern-day Balkh in North Afghanistan)
Titus	Greek Army Commander
Heliodorus	A Greek soldier
Brihadrath	King of Magadh of Maurya Dynasty
Pushyamitr	Army Chief of Magadh
Antonia	A Greek; wife of Titus
Batuk	A Nepali; former Indian soldier
Patanjali	Yoga Guru of Pushyamitr
Veersen	A Minister of Magadh
Sheelbhadr	A Minister of Magadh
Prajaamukh 1	People's Representative in the Magadh Court
Prajaamukh 2	People's Representative in the Magadh Court

Four Indian soldiers

6–8 Greek citizens

Musicians, Dancers, Drummers, Conch players, Umbrella bearer, Courtiers, etc. in the royal procession of King Brihadrath

'ONCE IN INDIA ': Photographs from an earlier production in India

Scene 1

CHARACTERS

Minender || Titus || Heliodorus ||
A bunch of Greek citizens

[*A Zeus temple in* Bactria, *where an idol/portrait of Zeus is in the center of the stage. Solemn religious music plays in the background. One torch is kept in front of the idol of Zeus. It highlights the mysterious darkness on the stage. Standing on one side of the idol is the Greek King Minender, and on the other side, a bunch of Greek citizens.*]

Minender: O Zeus! You are our heavenly God. Our Lord. Our protector. All other gods are thy servants. Zeus! We supplicants are standing before thee with bowed heads.

ALL: O Almighty One! Be kind to us. Protect us.

Minender: The sun shining in the sky, the stars and the moon, they are all circumambulating you, Zeus. The mountains, the roaring seas, the abundance of rich crops, the dry deserts, trees swinging in the air, the birds soaring high in the sky—these are all the miracles that you have created.

ALL: O Zeus! We are thy petitioners.

Minender: O Zeus! I, Minender, the King of Bactria, swear by you, making you the witness that there will be only your kingdom in India. Their gods and goddesses will lose their existence after you defeat them. The dream of Alexander the Great to conquer India remains unfulfilled. O Zeus! Kindly bless me to realize this dream.

ALL: Zeus! We are thy supplicants.

Minender: Our ancestors went to India with Alexander the Great to conquer that country. Alexander died on his way back to Greece due to the injuries he sustained there. He ascended to heaven with an unrealized dream in his heart. But most of my ancestors did not return to Greece. They stayed behind in Bactria to avenge the death of Alexander the Great and the defeat of the Greek General Seleucus Nicator. You have entrusted me with this responsibility. I swear by thy holy feet, I will discharge it faithfully.

ALL: O Zeus! We are thy servants.

Minender: Titus is going to India to execute the conquest of the country.
[*Titus comes forward and bows before the idol of Zeus.*]
He will lay down the foundation for Zeus' empire in India.
[*Titus kneels down.*]
O Zeus! He is kissing thy feet.

ALL: O Zeus! We are thy sheep.

Minender: Just as lemon curdles milk, Titus will weaken the might of India by creating a rift between the Vaidics and the Buddhists. And then, O Zeus, your slave Minender will attack India and Paataliputr to realize the dream of Alexander and Seleucus. O Zeus, bless thy slave to conquer India.

ALL: O Zeus! We are thy slaves.
[*All kneel down in prayer.*]

[SCENE FADES OUT]

SCENE 2

CHARACTERS

Titus || Heliodorus

[*In the spotlight on the front right corner of the stage, Heliodorus is seen standing with the maroon clothing of a Buddhist monk.*]

Titus: [*entering*] Heliodorus, where is my *cheever*? [*Heliodorus hands over the Buddhist garb to Titus, who puts it on over his Greek dress.*]

Titus: [*while wearing the Buddhist dress*] The bastards have detained one thousand Greek immigrants at the entrance gate to the city of Paataliputr. The soldiers have arrested them. My wife Antonia is amongst them.

Heliodorus: This is the mischief of that one man—that Pushyamitr Shung. So long as he remains the army chief of Magadh empire, he will not allow Zeus' Kingdom in this country.

Titus: He will have to be dealt with first. He is our enemy. Enemy number one.

Heliodorus: And Indians?

Titus: These Indian people, they are very greedy. Their eyes get blinded by the effulgence of gold. They cannot see anything beyond it. Throw some gold coins at every check-post; all hurdles will automatically get cleared away. But here in Paataliputr, Pushyamitr Shung's problem will have to be solved one day. [*In changed tone*] Where is the maalaa?
[*Heliodorus hands him the rosary.*]
Lo! I have become a Buddhist monk.
[*In lighter vein*] *"Buddham Sharanam Gacchaami"* (I take refuge in Buddha).

[SCENE FADES OUT]

SCENE 3

CHARACTERS

Brihadrath || Pushyamitr || Titus || Heliodorus

[Maurya King Brihadrath is sitting on a royal divan with his eyes closed in a meditative posture. Heliodorus is standing behind him as his bodyguard, with a lance.]

Pushyamitr: [*entering*] *Mahaaraaj*, I bow before your lotus feet.

Brihadrath: What brings our army chief here? Tell us, *Senaapati* Pushyamitr, what news have you brought?

Pushyamitr: The news is worrisome.

Brihadrath: Worrisome?

Pushyamitr: The Greek King Minender is preparing to invade India.

Brihadrath: You told us about this before.

Pushyamitr: Yes, but the latest intelligence further confirms the earlier reports.
[*King Brihadrath closes his eyes and goes into meditation.*]
The army of the Greek King was composed of Persians, Turks and Greeks. Now we've learned that they have also recruited ferocious tribesmen, the Pashtoons, to their forces. These Pashtoons trespass into our territories and indulge in plundering and killing innocent civilians. Our complaints to the Greek officials are of no avail. Instead, they made false counter allegations that it is we who are violating the boundary and indulging in acts of violence. [*Upon seeing the King in meditation*] Sorry, I will come some other time. *Mahaaraaj* is in meditation.

Brihadrath: [*with eyes closed*] Keep speaking, *Senaapati*, keep speaking. I am listening.

Pushyamitr: As you desire, Sir...

Brihadrath: [*opens his eyes*] *Senaapati*, I have taken birth into this world. But while doing everything that this world demands of me, my *dhyaan* always remains at the feet of Buddha.

Pushyamitr: I am aware of that, Sir.

Brihadrath: It is true that I am a King, but my heart does not rejoice in the battledrums of war. It is the *Dhamma-ghosh*, the trumpet of *Dharma*, that we Buddhists enjoy. I am a Chakravartee King, because I have turned the wheel of righteousness and taken refuge in Buddha. [*Changing his tone*] Now, continue with what you were saying.

Pushyamitr: The Greek King of Bactria is planning to attack India.

Brihadrath: I have heard this. What else do you have to say? [*He closes his eyes in meditation*].

Pushyamitr: *Mahaaraaj*, we will have to do something about it. History will not pardon us if we sit quietly. Destiny has entrusted the responsibility of protecting and defending this country to you. The aliens may attack us, destroy our homes, violate our women and hang our youth. It is better to commit suicide than to face such a possibility.

Brihadrath: [*opens his eyes*] No such thing will ever happen.

Pushyamitr: Sir...

Brihadrath: The Greeks will never attack us. I know this.

Pushyamitr: [*surrendering*] Certainly.

Brihadrath: What happens in the future, I come to know

beforehand. I hear an inner voice and get to know everything.

Pushyamittra: *Mahaaraaj*, you are great!

Brihadrath: Don't worry at all. [*Confidently*] Whatever I say is inviolable. It is bound to happen. [*He goes back into meditation.*]

Pushyamitr: [*hesitating*] There is one more piece of information, *Mahaaraaj*.

Brihadrath: [*opening his eyes*] What else is left to be said?

Pushyamitr: A group of one thousand Greek men and women, all illegal infiltrators, have entered India. They have reached the city's boundary, where they were accosted and arrested.

Brihadrath: [*shocked*] They have been arrested! But why? What is their crime? Have they killed someone? Was there any violence?

Pushyamitr: No. But they have arrived here illegally, by crossing our boundaries.

Brihadrath: What boundary? Did Buddha make these boundaries? They are neither guilty of bloodshed, nor of looting. Yet they have been subjected to the tor ure of prison! No…no…we cannot inflict such cruelty on non-violent people.

Pushyamitr: But they have entered illegally. They are infiltrators.
[*Titus enters.*]

Brihadrath: *Bhante* Aananda, come. You have arrived at an opportune time.

Titus: *Mahaaraaj*, what's the command?

Brihadrath: Our army chief is saying that a group of Greek immigrants has reached Paataliputr.

Pushyamitr: Illegally.

Titus: My sister is also part of that group.

Pushyamitr: Your sister, *Bhante*!

Titus: Yes, my sister Antonia.

Brihadrath: Your sister is imprisoned! This is grossly unfair. No, no, Pushyamitr. She will have to be released.

Pushyamitr: As commanded by *Mahaaraaj*, the sister of *Bhante*, Antonia, will be released.

Titus: What about the other Greeks? They have come seeking your refuge. Your *dharma* is to protect those who seek refuge with you.

Pushyamitr: If Greek infiltrators keep violating India's boundaries…

Titus: Where are the boundaries? There are no boundaries. Boundaries are imposed by the human heart. *Dharma* has no boundaries. Lord Buddha had said *Bahujan Hitaaye: Bahujan Sukhaaye*. "O monks! Go in all the four directions for the welfare and happiness of the people." There were no boundaries for Buddha. He commanded that we transcend the boundaries of all countries for the sake of humanity.

Pushyamitr: Many such settlements of illegal Greek immigrants have come up in the Maurya Empire. In every settlement, they have Greek temples. Every week, the Greeks assemble there...

Titus: Every week they assemble there to worship and receive the teachings of love, compassion, kindness and non-violence.

Pushyamitr: No, they go there to dream and plan a Greek takeover of India.

Titus: [*vehemently*] That's a lie.

Pushyamitr: This is the truth. This is the secret intelligence report, *Mahaaraaj*.

Titus: It is a false allegation. [*appealing*] *Mahaaraaj*! *Senaapati* is Indian and Vaidic. He hates us because we are Greeks and Buddhists.

Pushyamitr: [*draws his sword angrily*] If you speak one more word...[*He places the sword against Titus' chest.*] this sword will be in your chest.

[*Titus closes his eyes in fear and nervously moves the rosary quickly in his fingers.*]

For me, the Indians, the Greeks, the Buddhists, the Vaidics, the Braahmans, and the Shramans—

all are the same and equal. But above all is my country, the Mauryan empire. Defending the country is my foremost duty. I will destroy whosoever will come between me and my duty or make false allegations against me. I cannot accept a falsehood as a truth in order to appease anyone.
[*Silence for some time.*]

Brihadrath: I agree with you, *Senaapati. Dharm-mahaamaatra* Aananda has unwittingly accused you. Forget about it and release all the Greeks.

Pushyamitr: [*putting the sword back into the sheath*] The *Mahaaraaj's* orders will be carried out, but…

Brihadrath: But?

Pushyamitr: *Dharm-mahaamaatra* will have to apologize first.

Titus: My heart is full and overflowing with the milk of human kindness. Non-violence is my life. Nobody is Greek or Indian—Buddhist or Vaidic. All are one. They have the same grace of *Tathaagat*. Don't listen to words, *Senaapati*—look into my heart.

Pushyamitr: *Bhante!* Apologize.

Titus: My heart is brimming with compassion and love...

Pushyamitr: [*sternly*] Apologize.

Titus: [*nervously*] I apologize.
[*The King goes into meditation.*]

Pushyamitr: The orders of the King will be obeyed. All Greeks will be released. I beg your permission to leave.
[*He bows and exits.*]

[SCENE FADES OUT]

Scene 4

CHARACTERS

Titus || Antonia

[In the lighted area on the front right corner of the stage, Titus is seen standing in a Buddhist monk's attire. Antonia enters.]

Titus: [*with outstretched arms*] Antonia! Dear Antonia! [*Antonia merges into Titus arms.*] Welcome! Welcome!

Antoni: [*moving away from the embrace*]What are you wearing? These clothes…?

Titus: I am a Buddhist monk. Now my name is Aananda. I am the *Dharm-mahaamaatra* of the Mauryan empire.

Antonia: What does that mean?

Titus: It is a high office in the empire. As *Dharm-mahaamaatra*, it is my duty to ensure that everybody follows the path of *Dharma*. I am authorized to enter any house, shop, school or office without obstruction.

Antonia: How funny you look in these clothes! And what are you wearing underneath? Let me see. [*She proceeds to take off his clothes.*]

Titus: You are undressing me. Don't you feel shy?

Antonia: I am your wife. I can certainly undress you. [*She tries to take off his Buddhist gown.*]

Titus: Don't do this. I feel embarrassed. [*Antonia takes off his Buddhist garments. He is seen wearing the dress of a Greek soldier.*]

Antonia: This is my Titus. My Greek soldier! [*embracing him*] India has made you a billionaire. I have constructed a palace like that of kings in Bactria from the gold you've sent me from here. Did you find some buried treasure trove somewhere in India?

Titus: It is the miracle of this maroon dress.

Antonia: When will we return to Bactria?

Titus: Not now.

Antonia: But when? When will we live in our palace in

Bactria like a king and queen?

Titus: First, we will live like a king and queen here, in Paataliputr.

Antonia: [*astonished*] What are you saying?

Titus: Listen to me carefully. The King who sits on the throne of Paataliputr is a damned fool. An idiot of the first order. He is a fool and a hypocrite. He wants to show the world that after King Ashok, he is the only one who is as great.

Antonia: If that's what this King is like, why do the people not throw him out?

Titus: This is India. Indian people are very lazy. They tolerate everything, even injustice and tyranny. They similarly tolerate this idiot King. They not only tolerate him; they even worship him.

Antonia: What will you do?

Titus: I will not do anything. It is you who has to do something.

Antonia: Me? What can I do?

Titus: Beauty is the king's weakness. Any beautiful woman can ensnare him with her charms. I have not seen any other woman as voluptuous and enchanting as you are.

Antonia: So you think I am voluptuous and beautiful?

Titus: Without a doubt.

Antonia: More beautiful than all those women whom you keep chasing?

Titus: Definitely. More beautiful than all those women.

Antonia: Rest assured, your work will be done.

Titus: We Greeks do not have enough strength to avenge the defeat of Seleucus in the battlefield. But we have brains. We have cunningness. We have sowed the seeds of discord between the Buddhists and Vaidics. Slowly, the divide will widen. They will become suspicious of each other. They will mobilize against each other and become each others' enemies.

Antonia: Is this really possible?

Titus: Why not? I foresee the day when groups of Vaidics will come looking for Buddhists, and as soon as they find one, they will pounce upon him like hunting dogs. Buddhists will not remain quiet either. They will also come out with daggers concealed beneath their attire, and thrust them into the bodies of the Vaidics whom they encounter. The mixed blood of the Buddhists and Vaidics will flow onto the streets. The two will torch each others' houses. The darkness of death will be all around. I will...I will bring the doom of death into this country. [*with wild glee*] Then the army of the

Greek King Minender will arrive. Paataliputr will be under our occupation.

Antonia: Yes. One day, Greeks may occupy Paataliputr. But I want to know when Titus will occupy Antonia?

Titus: She will be occupied today. No, right now. [*Opening his belt, he moves towards her. She playfully runs away shouting "save me, save me" off-stage, with Titus chasing her.*]

[SCENE FADES OUT]

Scene 5

CHARACTERS

Titus || Brihadrath || Antonia

[Brihadrath is standing, with a prayer rosary in hand, on a higher level than Titus, who is in his audience.]

Titus: [*showing the letter in his hand*] The Greek King Minender has sent this letter to your Royal Highness.

Brihadrath: What does Minender write?

Titus: [*reading the letter*] Beloved of Zeus, the Greek King Minender warmly salutes the Indian King, who is the embodiment of *Dharma*, and the breeze of whose glory is flowing in our land.

Brihadrath: I accept his salutation. You may read further.

Titus: Yes. [*reading*] You are inspiring all men, animals, and even the birds of this world to move on the path of *'nirvaana,'* while carrying out their *karma*. You have opened schools, distributed money amongst the poor and food amongst the hungry of our country. All Greeks feel gratitude towards you. We want to install your statue in our capital. With your permission, a group of Greek sculptors will reach Paataliputr very soon to fashion a statue of you. All Greeks are your friends. Your friend forever and well-wisher, Beloved of Zeus, King Minender…

Brihadrath: The Greek King Minender wants to install my statue in his country?

Titus: He is seeking your auspicious presence in his country for good luck and blessings.

Brihadrath: Send him my consent. But there is one condition. There should be a canopy over the statue. I do not want birds over my head who may…

Titus: I understand. I will convey your royal wish. There is a letter from Upendra, our physician in Bactria.

Brihadrath: I believe that the hospitals maintained by us in the Greek capital are doing very well.

Titus: *Vaidya* Upendra has informed us that twenty thousand gold coins are immediately needed to keep running the hospital in Bactria.

Brihadrath: [*diffidently*] Pushyamitr questions why we should spend our gold on the Greeks. He asks if there are no poor in India?

Titus: It is a sin to look for mine and thine in acts of piety. When the sun rises, it does not see where its rays are reaching. It lights the world without any discrimination. Similarly, your compassion knows no limits. It's for the entirc humanity.

Brihadrath: [*suddenly remembering*] Antonia—is that not the name of your sister?

Titus: Yes, *Mahaabhaag*.

Brihadrath: You told me that she would come to meet us today.

Titus: She is here, outside, waiting for your permission.

Brihadrath: Then call her in.
[*Titus bows, exits and returns with Antonia. Antonia prostrates before the King, with her head touching the ground.*]

Brihadrath: Get up, Antonia, get up. Maurya Empire welcomes you.

Antonia: [*sitting down on her knees*] My long-held desire has been fulfilled. I feel blessed today. This is the reward of good *karmas* from many previous births.
[*Brihadrath gently gestures her to get up by touching her shoulders.*]

Antonia: *Mahaaraaj,* don't touch me. I am an ordinary

woman of this world—you are divine. I am not entitled to even touch your shadow.

Brihadrath: Don't say that. In this sorrow-filled world, the grace of *Tathaagat* is for everyone equally. Nobody is important or unimportant.

Antonia: I know, *Mahaaraaj*. I have studied the Buddhist scripture, *Tripitaka*. The teachings of *Tathaagat* resonate in my ears all the time.

Brihadrath: Can you read the Paalee language?

Antonia: Yes, *Mahaaraaj*. I have also studied the Sanskrit language...

Brihadrath: Wonderful. Do you know the names of the rivers of India?

Antonia: Yes, *Mahaaraaj*. Sindhu, Gangaa, Yamuna, Brahmaputra, Narmada, Krishna, Kaveri…

Brihadrath: And the mountains?

Antonia: Himaalaya, Vindhyaachal, Malayaachal, Mandaraachal, Mahendragiri…

Brihadrath: Amazing! Antonia, I have never seen as learned a woman as you. Aananda, you are fortunate that, by the grace of *Tathaagat*, you have such a brilliant sister. Brilliant as well as [*looking into Antonia's eyes*] beautiful.

Titus: *Mahaaraaj*, this is the kind grace of *Tathaagat*.

Brihadrath: [*to Antonia*] My Prime Minister passed away some time ago. I have not appointed anyone in his place yet.

Antonia: Why not, *Mahaaraaj*?

Brihadrath: I did not find anyone appropriate to appoint... but now I have found the right person.

Antonia: Then he should be appointed immediately. Who is he?

Brihadrath: You, Antonia.

Antonia: No *Mahaabhaag*! No! I am not worthy of this office. Kindly excuse me.

Brihadrath: I made the decision to appoint you as prime minister after deep contemplation.

Antonia: This is your greatness. But kindly excuse me.

Titus: Antonia, our King's desire is an order for us. We cannot disobey his order.

Antonia: I cannot dare to disobey the *Mahaabhaag's* orders. I am not even worth the dust of his feet. I can only petition. *Mahaaraaj*, be kind and release me of the responsibility. [*She sits on her knees with folded hands.*] I am not worthy of this office.

Brihadrath: Alright, Antonia. I release you from my orders. [*Antonia respectfully bows before him.*]

You have renounced such a great honor! Antonia, history would know you as Saint Antonia.

Antonia: *Mahaabhaag*, before going I want to make a request of you.

Brihadrath: What is it?

Antonia: Before leaving for India, I saw a flash of light during my meditation in Gaandhaar, then…

Brihadrath: Then, what?

Antonia: Then, I saw a divine image.

Brihadrath: A divine image! Of whom?

Antonia: I did not know then, but when I saw you today, I immediately knew that it was you, *Mahaabhaag*, who had come to bless me in my meditation.

Titus: *Mahaaraaj* is omnipresent. He is in many places at the same time. You have been specially blessed by him.

Antonia: I have only one request to make of *Mahaabhaag*.

Brihadrath: What is it?

Antonia: I am such a lowly person. I feel hesitant to make a request of such a god-like King.

Brihadrath: Don't hesitate. Make your request.

Titus: Why don't you speak? *Mahaaraaj* has given you permission.

Antonia: *Mahaabhaag*, I want to meditate in your kind presence so that I may be blessed by the vibrations emerging from your meditation.

Brihadrath: I accept your request.
[*Antonia bows and Brihadrath raises his hand, blessing her.*]

[SCENE FADES OUT]

SCENE 6

CHARACTERS

Antonia || Brihadrath

[Brihadrath is sitting on a divan in meditation with his eyes closed. Antonia is sitting nearby in meditation on the floor.]

Antonia: [*opening her eyes*] *Mahaabhaag*!
[*Brihadrath opens his eyes.*]
The waves from your meditation are not reaching me. You are too far. If you permit, I will come a little closer to you.

Brihadrath: Permitted.
[*Antonia moves a little closer to the King. Both resume meditation.*]

Antonia: [*opening her eyes after a little while*] *Mahaabhaag*!

Brihadrath: Now what happened?

Antonia: I am still too far from you. The waves from your meditation are still not able to reach me.

Brihadrath: You may come closer.
[*Antonia sits near Brihadrath and closes her eyes.*]

Antonia: *Mahaabhaag*, do you know about *Shaktipaat*...I mean, about transmitting energy? If you put your right hand on my head, the flow of energy will be from your body into mine.

Brihadrath: Alright. Come closer to me. Here, come and sit down.
[*Antonia sits on the floor near Brihadrath's feet. He puts his right hand on her head.*]

Antonia: [*with eyes closed*] Oh, what a divine experience! It feels like a fountain of electric sparks is emanating from your hand. The electric sparks are slowly, very slowly, descending down my body—first my head, then forehead, eyes, nose, lips, chin, neck, breasts and further down, down. Oh no! I cannot bear it. This will burn me up!

Brihadrath: This fire is burning me too. Come here, Antonia. Sit next to me on the couch.
[*Antonia sits on the couch, close to the King. Their shoulders touch.*]

Antonia: Now it's fine. I am receiving full energy from your body.

[*Both Antonia and Brihadrath close their eyes in meditation.*]

Brihadrath: [*suddenly getting up*] Attack! Attack!

Antonia: What happened?

Brihadrath: The royal palace of Paataliputr has been attacked.

Antonia: Attacked! Who has attacked?

Brihadrath: *Maar* has attacked. *Tathaagat* conquered *Maar*. I will also have to conquer *Maar*.

Antonia: Who is *Maar*?

Brihadrath: He is the god of desire, of sex.

Antonia: Where is he? [*looking around*] I don't see him anywhere.

Brihadrath: He can't be seen, but he is here. He is all-around.

Antonia: How does *Maar* look? Is he a giant, with big fang-like teeth and big nails?

Brihadrath: No.

Antonia: Then what does he look like?

Brihadrath: He appears in the bodies of various charming women. Each woman more beautiful than the last. More luscious and delicious than the nymphets of Paradise, with dark cloud-like black hair, eyes like two fish dancing in a blue lake, ruby-red soft cheeks, lips with the smile of flower buds, silky arms like that of a lotus-stem and and two black bees sitting over two blooming white lotus flowers. Antonia, the beauty of *Maar* is very terrifying. [*The palm of his right hand suddenly starts closing and opening involuntarily.*]

Antonia: *Mahaabhaag*, what is happening to your hand?

Brihadrath: [*looking at his hand*] I don't know. I am trying my best to control it. [*He stops the involuntary movement of his right hand by holding it with his left.*] Look, it has stopped. [*As soon as he releases his right hand from the grip of his left hand, its involuntary movement returns again.*] I think it wants to hold something.

Antonia: Wants to hold something?

Brihadrath: Yes.

Antonia: I will bring something. [*She goes off-stage and returns with a sword.*] Here it is. *Mahaabhaag*, you may hold the sword.
[*Brihadrath tries to hold the sword in his right hand, but is unable to do so. It slips out of his hand.*]

Antonia: *Mahaabhaag*, I am a great fool. You are a votary of non-violence, and I gave you a sword. Sorry, I will bring something else. [*She goes off-stage *with the sword and returns with a book.*]

Brihadrath: The book seems to be alright.

Antonia: *Mahaaraaj*, now hold the book. Everything will be alright.
[*Brihadrath tries to hold the book, but it too slips out of his hand.*]

Antonia: Now, what should I put into your restless hand to hold? *Mahaabhaag*, you may hold my hand.
[*She extends her hand. Brihadrath catches hold of her wrist with his right hand.*]

Brihadrath: [*triumphantly*] Look, my hand has stopped moving.

Antonia: [*coquettishly*] Oh yes. [*She pulls out her hand from his grip. The involuntary movement of Brihadrath's hand returns again.*]

Brihadrath: [*looking at his hand*] My hand!

Antonia: Let it be as it is. I will not give you my hand.

Brihadrath: [*imploring*] Antonia!

Antonia: Your hands are shameless and obstinate.

Brihadrath: [*looking at the opening and closing of his hand and helplessly appealing*] Antonia, please.

Antonia: [*faking unwillingness*] You are very demanding.

Here, hold my hand.

Brihadrath: [*holding her hand*] See, my hands have stopped moving.

Antonia: [*suddenly holds him in her arms*] Let there be the descent of electric sparks in my body.

[SCENE FADES OUT]

Scene 7

CHARACTERS

Brihadrath || Antonia

[Brihadrath is sitting on his throne while Antonia is standing near him.]

Brihadrath: [*addressing his courtiers*] Honorable Courtiers, Reverend *Dharm-mahaamaatra* Aananda, *Senaapati* Pushyamitr Shung! We have summoned this assembly for an important declaration. My father-like Prime Minister went to his heavenly abode last month. He was also the Prime Minister of my late father, King Shat Dhanush. Who should I appoint in place of an experienced, knowledgeable, competent, and faithful Prime Minister? This was a problem I faced. This problem was automatically solved when, by the grace of *Tathaagat,* we met Aaryaa Antonia. She has mastery over the Paalee and Sanskrit languages. She is an authority on *Tripitaka.* She is a scholar of grammar, astronomy, administration, geography and diplomacy. She has done a special study of *Arthshastra* of Kautily. She has many qualities that I have known and personally tested. Today, I appoint her the Prime Minister of the Magadh empire.

[*Sounds of conch shells are heard from off-stage. Antonia bows with folded hands to the sound of clapping.*]

[SCENE FADES OUT]

SCENE 8

CHARACTERS

Titus ‖ Antonia ‖ Batuk

[On the front right corner of the stage Titus stands in the spotlight. Antonia enters from the opposite side.]

Titus: [*with open arms*] Welcome to the Prime Minister of the Maurya Empire. [*He playfully bows before her.*]

Antonia: You asked me to snare the King, that damn fool, and I have done that.

Titus: How did you find the victim of femme fatale? I hope you did not fall in love with your prey?

Antonia: What nonsense, Titus!

Titus: If the Prime Minister ever thought of becoming the Queen of Magadh, [*takes out his dagger*] by Zeus, this dagger would be in your body.

Antonia: You're jealous. I won't go back there. I'll resign from this post.

Titus: I did not mean…

Antonia: [*angrily*] As I said, I will not go. I'll not go back to him.

Titus: [*appeasing*] Try to understand me. I did not mean to hurt you.

Antonia: It is you who asked me to go to him. I went to him only for you.

Titus: I did not ask you to go there for myself. I sent you there for Zeus—for Greece. We have to realize the unfulfilled dream of Alexander the Great. We have to avenge the defeat of Seleucus Nicator.

Antonia: My dear Titus, I have all the fun in the world. Swing in love with him, and lo you have served Greece. Which woman would not like to be such a patriot!

Titus: I would like you to meet Batuk.
[*Titus goes off-stage and returns with Batuk.*]

Titus: This is Batuk. He comes from Nepal. Poor soul. Batuk is an orphan. He was in the army. Due to an accidental injury, he lost his speech and his job too. Now he is unemployed, with no source of income.

Antonia: [*sympathizing*] Poor Batuk! When were you injured? How long ago?

Titus: He cannot hear. He is deaf, too. Due to the head injury, he became both deaf and dumb. I have chosen him for your security. He will always accompany you, and he will not be able to hear our conversations.

Antonia: I bow to you. Your mind is the abode of the devil.

Titus: He can read. If you want to tell him something, give it to him in writing. He will understand. He is an expert in wielding weapons. He will show you.
[*Titus gestures to Batuk to touch the feet of Antonia as a mark of respect. Batuk touches her feet. Then Titus gives him his dagger and gestures to him to demonstrate dagger-wielding. Batuk shows his proficiency in wielding a dagger.*]

Antonia: [*clapping*] Good. Very good. Batuk is an expert warrior.

[SCENE FADES OUT]

SCENE 9

CHARACTERS

Brihadrath || Titus || Veersen || Batuk || Pushyamitr || Antonia || Sheelbhadr

[Brihadrath's royal court. Brihadrath is sitting on the throne. Batuk is standing behind him with a lance to guard him. Dharm-mahaamaatra Aananda, Prime Minister Antonia, Ministers Sheelbhadr and Veersen, and Senaapati Pushyamitr are sitting in their seats.]

Brihadrath: I have summoned this assembly at the request of *Senaapati* Pushyamitr. He has some proposals, some suggestions. I want you to consider them. *Senaapati*, you may submit your suggestions before the assembly.

Pushyamitr: [*standing up*] Honorable Courtiers! Today,

we are in a critical phase of history. Our one decision, whether right or wrong, will determine the future course of our history.

Brihadrath: Submit your suggestion without any background.

Pushyamitr: [*pointing to Batuk*] In his presence?

Brihadrath: He is deaf and dumb. Submit your case.

Pushyamitr: The Greek King can invade India anytime now.

Titus: That's impossible.

Pushyamitr: [*sternly*] *Dharm-mahaamaatra* Aananda! Let me finish what I have to say. Our army is not prepared for war.

Antonia: Why is it not prepared for war? The army is being paid a regular salary.

Pushyamitr: Their weapons are outmoded and obsolete. The swords used a hundred years ago at the time of King Ashok during the Kaling conquest are still being used and have rusted. During the last hundred years, their headgears and armors have neither been repaired nor changed.

Brihadrath: *Senaapati*, you have had your say. Does anyone else have anything else to say about this? How about you, Veersen?

Veersen: How much would it cost to re-equip the army?

Pushyamitr: About two hundred thousand.

Antonia: Two hundred thousand! Minister Sheelbhadr, do we have this amount in the Royal Treasury?

Sheelbhadr: This is a large amount. About a month ago, thirty thousand gold coins were sent abroad for the propagation of *Dharma* in Minender's Greek Kingdom.

Antonia: If such a large amount is not in the Royal Treasury, what can be done? *Senaapati*, we may have to postpone purchasing army equipment as of now.

Titus: But why is there a need to equip the army?

Pushyamitr: [*ignoring Titus*] If this amount cannot be released all at once, can it be provided in instalments?

Antonia: What do you mean?

Pushyamitr: Twenty thousand may be released immediately, the rest in due time.

Titus: But my basic question remains unanswered. Why should the army be equipped?

Pushyamitr: Because we have an army.

Titus: Why do we have an army?

Pushyamitr: Because the Greek King Minender has an army.

Titus: Shall we do all that the Greek King does?

Pushyamitr: We should do everything that all kings do.

Titus: All kings wage wars. But King Ashok did not wage any war after the Kaling conquest. After him, no Maurya King ever waged a war. [*pointing to Brihadrath*] Our *Mahaabhaag*, too, did not wage war. So for what purpose do we need an army? We do not need an army.

Pushyamitr: [*defiantly*] We need an army for defense, not for aggression.

Titus: Defense? Defense from whom? *Senaapati*, you do not know the power of non-violence. That's why you talk about weapons and army.

Pushyamitr: [*ironically*] *Dharm-Mahamatra*! I am merely a soldier. True, I am not aware of the power of non-violence. Perhaps you may kindly teach it to me.

Titus: When soldiers of the King failed to arrest the killer Angulimaal as their weapons proved ineffective, Lord Buddha himself went without any weapons, armed with non-violence…and Angulimaal fell at the feet of Buddha .

Pushamitra: That was in ancient times. Who has such Buddha-like power today? I don't see anyone like that.

Titus: Never say that again. Even today, we have amongst us, a mighty powerhouse of non-violence. At his feet, not one, but many Angulimaals may surrender.

Pushyamitr: Who is that?

Titus: [*pointing to Brihadrath*] Our King, the embodiment of *Dharma*, the ruler of Magadh.

Pushyamitr: [*politely*] The Greek King has completed all his preparations to invade India...The spies from the Northwest are continually sending such reports. [*appealing*] *Mahaaraaj*, would we welcome the Greeks when they invade us?

Brihadrath: What you are saying is based on intelligence reports that you have received. Prime Minister Antonia has set up a parallel agency to collect intelligence. According to her agency's reports, the Greeks are preparing to attack *Paarseeks* in Iran, not India.
[*Pushyamitr gives up and sits down.*]

Titus: Why would they attack India? They are grateful to India. We send them hundreds of thousands of gold coins to run hospitals, schools, construct wells and roads, and to distribute amongst the poor.

Brihadrath: Minender is our friend, our well-wisher.

Titus: [*to Veersen*] The group of Greek sculptors will be reaching Paataliputr shortly. They will be making a statue of our King to be installed in the city square at Gaandhaar.

Veersen: It's something to be proud of—a statue of our King amongst the Greeks!

Titus: The *Mahaaraaj's* glory has reached beyond our frontiers into distant lands.

Antonia: *Mahaaraaj* may kindly recall the letter of our physician from Gaandhaar. He has asked for twenty thousand gold coins. If you permit, this amount may be sent to him.

Pushyamitr: [*angrily*] No *Mahaaraaj*! Our people should not be starved to feed aliens. First equip the army, then give to charity. I am firm in my conviction. [*He walks out.*]

[*Brihadrath sees the army chief walking out from the court but does not react. Instead, he closes his eyes and goes into meditation.*]

[SCENE FADES OUT]

SCENE 10

CHARACTERS

Antonia ‖ Brihadrath ‖ Batuk ‖ Pushyamitr ‖ Titus

[Brihadrath is sitting on a divan in his private chamber. Batuk is massaging his neck and shoulders. Antonia enters.]

Antonia: Did you hear? Around midnight yesterday, someone broke into the Zeus temple and tried to put the altar on fire.

Brihadrath: I know.

Antonia: *Bhante* Aananda tried to put out the fire, but the miscreants attacked his head. He fell down unconscious. His head is injured and he bled a lot.

Brihadrath: I had sent the state physician to him this morning. How is he now? Can he move around?

Antonia: Yes, he can walk without support. But his head injury is very serious. He has a bandage around his head. I am not concerned just because he is my brother. My heart cannot bear the suffering of anyone, not even of animals and plants.

Brihadrath: I know your heart is full of compassion for all living beings. I have heard the beatings of your heart many times before.

Antonia: It is definitely the doing of the Army Chief Pushyamitr Shung. He neither likes Greeks, nor Buddhists. If allowed his way, he would drown them all in the river Gangaa, and shout in his Vaidic way *Har Har Gange.*

Brihadrath: You say that miscreants set the Zeus temple on fire around midnight?

Antonia: Yes, Sir. The curtains have been burnt. The wooden frame of a door also caught fire.

Brihadrath: Yesterday evening, six hours before the incident, the Army Chief sent me the intelligence report that some Greek leaders have conspired to set their own temple on fire.

Antonia: Why? Why would the Greeks arson their own temple?

Brihadrath: So that they may arouse the sympathy of common people, and malign the army and its chief, Pushyamitr Shung.

Antonia: *Mahaaraaj,* I understand. It just dawned on me. This conspiracy was hatched by the army chief himself. In the evening, he sent the intelligence report to *Mahaaraaj* that Greeks would set fire the Zeus temple at midnight, and then organized his men to set it on fire at midnight. [*emphatically*] *Mahaaraaj*, this is all Pushyamitr Shung's mischief.

Brihadrath: I have sent for Pushyamitr, and also for *Bhante* Aananda. They might be sitting outside. Call them in.

Antonia: [*to Batuk*] Batuk, ask the army chief and *Bhante* to come in.

[*Batuk does not respond.*]

Antonia: [*to herself*] I always forget that he's deaf and dumb. I will go myself.

[*Antonia goes out and returns with Titus and Pushyamitr. Titus' head is wrapped in a bandage. He walks in with Antonia's support.*]

Brihadrath: Oh *Bhante*! You are severely injured.

Titus: Don't worry about me. In my previous birth, I must have injured someone and this is the return of that *karma*.

Brihadrath: *Bhante*, I am unable to understand why anyone would arson the Zeus temple. The Greeks are such peaceful citizens.

Titus: One of the four noble truths propounded by

Lord Buddha is that life is full of suffering. This is the misdeed of some ignorant and misguided people. I have forgiven them. You may also kindly forgive them.

Brihadrath: Who should be forgiven? I should first at least know the name of the culprit, so that he may be forgiven.

Titus: Whoever he may be, I have forgiven him.

Brihadrath: I have not forgiven him. He should be punished.

Titus: Punishment is also violence. We non-violent Buddhist monks only know forgiveness and non-violence.

Pushyamitr: My intelligence team informed me in advance about the Greek conspiracy to arson the Zeus temple.

Brihadrath: It is also possible that you yourself got the temple set on fire, but to shift the blame onto the Greeks you had the intelligence report sent in advance.

Pushyamitr: Yes. This is also possible, *Mahaaraaj*. It needs to be investigated.

Brihadrath: *Bhante*, what do you have to say in this regard?

Titus: The inquiry is unnecessary. I have already forgiven the culprit. My mind is at the feet of *Tathaagat.* Let it remain there.

Pushyamitr: If my people had set the temple on fire, *Bhante* Aananda's head would be injured. If the Greeks had set the fire themselves, there would be no injury to his head.

Brihadrath: How can we find this out?

Pushyamitr: By opening the bandage on *Bhante's* head.

Brihadrath: [*to Titus*] Do you agree, *Bhante*?

Antonia: [*vehemently interjecting*] I do not agree.

Brihadrath: Prime Minister, why do you object?

Antonia: It would sully your image and glorious fame. You cannot give such an order.

Brihadrath: Why not?

Antonia: *Mahaaraaj*, if you give such an order to *Bhante*, it would mean you do not trust him. And if this is so, then why did you appoint such an unreliable person onto *Dharm-mahaamaatra's* post? It puts a question mark on *Mahaaraaj's* wisdom. If people come to know about it, their loyalty and devotion to their King will be compromised. No, *Mahaaraaj*, you should not give such an order.
[*Brihadrath falls into deep thought.*]

Pushyamitr: Prime Minister, you are very sharp, but I am awaiting the *Mahaaraaj's* order. [*He sits down.*]

Brihadrath: Who am I to decide between *Senaapati* and *Bhante*? Who is truthful and who is not? The truth is like the sun. When the truth emerges, it illumines the whole world with its light. As soon as the sun appears, the darkness hides itself in the nooks and corners of caves. One day, the truth will definitely shine like the sun. Let us wait for that day. [*He closes his eyes, and goes into meditation.*]

[SCENE FADES OUT]

Scene 11

CHARACTERS

Batuk || Titus || Antonia

[On the front right corner of the stage, Batuk is seen handcuffed. Titus enters with a whip in his right hand, and a cup of wine in his left. There is no bandage on his head.]

Titus: Batuk, I ask you for the last time—are you in league with Pushyamitr?

[*Batuk is unable to hear. Titus writes his question on a slate and shows it to Batuk.*]

Batuk, read it and tell me if you are with Pushyamitr?

[*Batuk denies it by shaking his head vigorously.*]

Titus: Lie! Absolute lie!! [*He whips Batuk with wild vehemence.*]

Titus: [*whipping him severely*] Bastard! You son of a bitch!
[*Antonia enters.*]

Antonia: Did he confess?

Titus: The dog is silent so far. He does not bark.

Antonia: If he didn't leak our plan to set fire to the Zeus temple, then who else could have done it?

Titus: No one else. It is this bastard who leaked it.

Antona: Titus, when we planned to set fire to the Zeus temple there was no one except him. But he is deaf. He can't hear.

Titus: He can hear. He certainly can hear. If he didn't hear, then how did our plan get out? He is only pretending to be deaf and dumb. I will take all this nonsense out of him. [*He whips Batuk.*]

Antonia: Titus, leave him to me. Let me talk to him. You go.

Titus: Alright. You may also try. [*He goes out.*]

Antonia: [*sympathizing*] Oh my God! Your back is badly bruised. Titus is a very cruel and vicious man. He will kill you. But I can save you. I can protect you. Believe me, I'll protect you. You remind me of my younger brother. I am like your sister. I will protect you. Yes...I will

protect my younger brother.
[*Batuk does not respond.*]
I don't really believe that you are deaf. If you were deaf, then the plan that Titus and I conceived would not have reached a third person. You were undoubtedly listening. I am telling you, finally, if you come out with the truth, we will forgive you. We Greeks also believe in forgiveness. Really, we will forgive you. Just tell the truth once. [*Suddenly stamping her feet, she flares up in a rage.*] Speak the truth, or else, be prepared to die. [*calling out*] Titus!
[*Titus enters.*]

Antonia: I failed. He does not speak up. Now, he's at your disposal.

Titus: Should he be killed or let off?

Antonia: Killed.

Titus: He is an Indian and Vaidic...

Antonia: Doubly poisonous. In my childhood, I had heard a saying: "if one comes across a snake and a *Vaidic* Indian, the *Vaidic* Indian should be killed first."

Titus: He has betrayed us. Today, I will sacrifice him in the name of Zeus.

Antonia: No Titus. This sacrifice is on my behalf. Give me your dagger.

[*Titus hands over the dagger to Antonia.*]

Antonia: [*raising the dagger*] In the name of Zeus [*is about to stab Batuk*]...

Batuk: Stop!

Titus: The dumb has spoken out in the face of death!

Antonia: Life is dear to everyone.

Batuk: I do not want to save my life.

Antonia: [*ironically*] Really!

Batuk: Before dying, I want to tell you that you will never succeed in your mission.

Titus: [*taunting*] What else do you want to tell me before your death?

Batuk: That the dream of Alexander to conquer India will never be realized. You will not be able to avenge the defeat of Seleucus.

Titus: Why not?

Batuk: Hundreds of thousands of youth have sworn to sacrifice their lives in defense of their motherland.

Titus: You people regard the earth of this country as your mother. You want to sacrifice your life for your motherland. [*He takes the dagger from*

Antonia's hands.] I will fulfill your desire, Batuk! [*He is about to stab Batuk.*]

Batuk: My name is not Batuk. My name is Buddhapriya.

Titus: [*taken aback*] What! You're Buddhist?

Batuk: Yes.

Titus: I am also a Buddhist. We are friends of Buddhists. We have no quarrel with them. Our quarrel is with the Vaidic people. Why are you against us if you are a Buddhist?

Batuk: I am against you because I am a Buddhist.

Titus: What have we done?

Batuk: Nothing could be more lowly and hateful than what you have done. You people are sullying the fair name of Lord Buddha by your dark deeds. You are committing fraud, conspiracy, and murders under the cover of His name. You are demeaning Buddhism by your evil deeds.

Antonia: He is full of venom.

Batuk: Titus, we may be Buddhists or Vaidics, but we are all Indians. This land is the mother of all of us. No foreigner can take over our motherland. We are all prepared. The eye that see us with enmity will be plucked out. The hands that attack us will be amputated. The legs of enemies marching towards us will be cut off.

Antonia: That's enough. [*She snatches the dagger from Titus and thrusts it into Batuk's chest, who then collapses.*]

Antonia: Long live Zeus!

Titus: Long live Alexander! Long live Seleucus!

[SCENE FADES OUT]

SCENE 12

CHARACTERS

Pushyamitr ‖ Soldier 1 ‖ Soldier 2

[Two soldiers bring over Batuk's dead body which is covered with a sheet of cloth and place it on the ground. Pushyamitr enters. He removes the cloth from Batuk's face but quickly puts it back. He gets up and fights hard to conceal his grief.]

Pushyamitr: [*in an emotion-choked voice*] My most trusted and reliable soldier has passed away. [*to the Soldiers*] Where did you find his dead body?

Soldier 1: Along the banks of the river Gangaa.

Pushyamitr: Where on the banks of the Gangaa? The banks of the Gangaa are very large. The entire city of Paataliputr is on the banks of the Gangaa.

Soldier 1: [*nervously*] I meant to say…

Pushyamitr: How far from the Zeus temple?

Soldier 2: Not very far from the Zeus temple. Hardly half a mile away.

Pushyamitr: On the banks of the Gangaa. In the sands near the water?

Soldier 2: No, Sir. A little away from the river stream. Under the cluster of trees.

Pushyamitr: [*thinking aloud*] If the killers carried the body to the river, why did they not throw it into the river?

Soldier 1: They could not do so.

Pushyamitr: Why not?

Soldier 1: Today is the Gangaa-bathing festival. On the banks of the Gangaa, the crowd of bathers had started collecting before dawn. For this reason, it seems, the killers could not throw the body into the river. They ran away after leaving the dead body in the darkness, under the cluster of trees.

Pushyamitr: I know who those murderers were. I know who killed Buddhapriya. His sacrifice will not go waste. I swear by the pious river Gangaa to destroy Buddhapriya's murderers.

[SCENE FADES OUT]

SCENE 13

CHARACTERS

Brihadrath || Antonia

[King Brihadrath's bedroom. Brihadrath is reclining in bed on top of pillows. Antonia is massaging his feet.]

Brihadrath: The magic of your beauty has made me your slave.

Antonia: You are not a slave. It's me who is the slave. That's why I am massaging your feet.

Brihadrath: I did not ask you to. You are massaging my feet on your own.
[*Antonia stops massaging Brihadrath's feet and gets up.*]

Brihadrath: What happened?

Antonia: I am not your slave anymore.

Brihadrath: That's right, you are not my slave. You are my lovely, lovely bed-partner.

Antonia: A few moments ago I was your bed-partner, but now I am not. Now, I am the Prime Minister of Maurya empire.

Brihadrath: My bed-partner, as well as the Prime Minister!

Antonia: Yes.

Brihadrath: How can a woman be both at the same time?

Antonia: Why not?

Brihadrath: How?

Antonia: Listen—when I am your bed-partner, I am not your Prime Minister. And when I am Prime Minister, I am not your bed-partner.

Brihadrath: Understood. But how would I know when my doe-eyed, dear, dear Antonia is my bed-partner, and when she is the Prime Minister?

Antonia: This, of course, you should know. After all, you have seen and explored me so much!

Brihadrath: Understood. Now you are the Prime Minister. Tell me, what are your orders for this King?

Antonia: The Prime Minister does not give orders to the King, she advises.

Brihadrath: Then what is her advice for the King?

Antonia: The Prime Minister is unhappy to see that the army chief insults the King. He is arrogant. He dares to argue with the King.

Brihadrath: No. It is not so.

Antonia: If he doesn't insult, then he definitely disobeys the King.

Brihadrath: He is my childhood friend. His father was also my father's army chief.

Antonia: He should at least sometimes obey you. Twenty thousand gold coins have to be sent for our hospitals in Gaandhaar and Bactria, but could not be sent due to his objection.

Brihadrath: I myself have not given the order so far. If I decide to order this, the army chief will definitely comply.

Antonia: Then give the orders. What are you waiting for? The Prime Minister should know that the army chief is loyal to his King.

Brihadrath: Alright. I will give orders. [*taking her earrings in his fingers*] Your earrings are very beautiful. When the vermillion of your cheeks glows in the golden hue of your earrings, I am reminded of the song…

Antonia: You are a big liar. [*She playfully hits Brihadrath's chest with her fists.*]

Brihadrath: Now what happened?

Antonia: You promised to get me a necklace and bangles from Mysore to match these earrings.

Brihadrath: [*assuringly*] I will get them soon.

Antonia: When will that soon be? When I am old? When I will move with a stick in my hand?

Brihadrath: My Antonia will never get old. Just as old wine gets more intoxicating with time, so will my Antonia's beauty.

Antonia: [*suddenly*] How has this happened! The Prime Minister was here. From where has your bed-partner suddenly emerged?

Brihadrath: [*defensively*] I didn't call her.

Antonia: Your bed-partner is very shameless. She comes uninvited. The Prime Minister has not yet finished her discussions of state matters.

Brihadrath: My bed-partner, you must go. You may come back when invited. I have to discuss urgent matters with the Prime Minister. Come, Prime Minister. My bed-partner has left. Honorable Prime Minister of Maurya Empire may come in.

Antonia: [*announcing gleefully*] The Prime Minister has

arrived.

Brihadrath: [*playfully*] What's your command, Madam Prime Minister?

Antonia: [*suddenly serious*] This is not a joke. Listen to me carefully. All over the world, the flag of Mauryan glory is unfurling. Do you know why?

Brihadrath: You tell me.

Antonia: Because the Mauryan empire has no enemies. The Buddhist monasteries established by it are serving the poor and orphaned in distant lands. The kings ruling far and wide regard you as the reincarnation of Lord Buddha. Would the nations that are burdened with the weight of your generosity ever attack you?

Brihadrath: Never.

Antonia: Then why should the money be wasted on the army equipment? If this amount is spent on the welfare of the people of the world, the spiritual merit will accrue to the King.

Brihadrath: [*thinking*] But...

Antonia: Why did King Ashok declare not to wage wars in the future? Why did he choose to turn the wheel of *Dharma*, instead of beating the drums of war? Only for the sake of this spiritual merit. Then why do you step back from the call of *Dharma*? Is it out of fear of that one man...that army chief?

Brihadrath: He has the army. He is the army chief.

Antonia: But the army is with you. They are devoted to their King. Just dare once, and say boldly in the assembly of courtiers that since we do not have any enemy, there is no need for the army. Reduce the army's strength by one-fourth. I will manage all the members of the Royal Court.

Brihadrath: [*seeking reassurance*] You will be able to manage?

Antonia: A hundred per cent.

Brihadrath: Alright then. I will order accordingly.

Antonia: Lo, the Prime Minister has gone. Your bed-partner has returned.

Brihadrath: Welcome my bed-partner! [*Antonia merges in his embrace.*]

[SCENE FADES OUT]

SCENE 14

CHARACTERS

Patanjali || Pushyamitr

[On the front left corner of the stage, Patanjali is seen seated on a low seat with his eyes closed in meditation. Pushyamitr enters, unarmed and dressed in simple white upper and lower garments.]

Pushyamitr: Pushyamitr bows at Gurudev's lotus feet.

Patanjali: Be victorious. How did you come?

Pushyamitr: My intense desire to seek your blessings has brought me today.

Patanjali: The Guru's blessings! Does the army chief have

so much spare time to seek this?

Pushyamitr: The army chief has all the time now. He will now complete yoga lessons from his Guru . He will withdraw from the affairs of this material world to realize the next step of meditation and enter the stage of Samaadhi, the eternal bliss.

Patanjali: What am I hearing! Ignoring the concerns of the country and the nation, Pushyamitr is seeking Samaadhi?

Pushyamitr: Salvation is the goal of all human beings. It's mine too.

Patanjali: No. Salvation is not your goal. You are not an individual. You have an obligation towards all the people of this nation. You are responsible for the salvation of millions of Indians.

Pushyamitr: What can I do? I'm helpless. I have received an intelligence report that Antonia and Titus are conspiring to dismantle one-fourth of the army. They have also involved other Ministers and Courtiers in the conspiracy.

Patanjali: How is this possible?

Pushyamitr: They bribed them. It is difficult to resist the glitter of gold.

Patanjali: And the King?

Pushyamitr: Antonia's magic has bewitched King Brihadrath. The King regards himself as half

Greek. He claims that he has the blood of his ancestor Chandragupt, who defeated the Greek General Seleucus and married his daughter. Thus, he has blood ties with Greeks. It is for this reason that he is not prepared to believe that the Greeks can ever invade India.

Patanjali: What has the army chief decided?

Pushyamitr: The demoralized Mauryan army will not be able to resist the Greek army's invasion with their outmoded weapons. Thousands of our soldiers will be killed. The rest of the soldiers will run away from the battlefield for their lives.

Patanjali: What is the army chief's role in this?

Pushyamitr: I am foreseeing cruel bloodshed. The Greeks' blood-thirsty swords slashing the necks of Indians. Men, women, young and old—nobody escapes the mayhem. The chopped heads are rolling around. The Greek soldiers' blood-stained shoes are advancing on this pious land to enslave it. Greeks are setting fire to Indian homes. Those trying to escape are being hunted down by Greek lancers. The Indian women are shrieking. There is nobody to save their honor.

Patanjali: [*angrily*] Where is the army chief?

Pushyamitr: Away from this worldly turmoil, far away, in a cave of some mountain, enjoying the eternal bliss of deep Samaadhi.

Patanjali: Patanjali is ashamed of his disciple.

Pushyamitr: [*vehemently*] Is it not the duty of the army chief to obey the orders of his King? To be loyal to his master?

Patanjali: Are you loyal to the King or to the country?

Pushyamitr: [*thinking*] Perhaps to both.

Patanjali: If you have to choose between the two?

Pushyamitr: I am bound by oath to be loyal to the King...

Patanjali: Loyalty to the King is your personal loyalty. Loyalty to the country is greater than loyalty to the King.

Pushyamitr: What should I do?

Patanjali: You should choose your own path.

Pushyamitr: How can I succeed in proving my loyalty to the nation when one-fourth of the army is retrenched? How can the demoralized army defend this nation without weapons and equipment?

Patanjali: I will not answer you. You will have to find the answer for this yourself. [*Closes his eyes in meditation.*]

[*Pushyamitr remains standing, confused for some time.*]

Pushyamitr: [*to himself*] Should I break my oath of loyalty to the King? Should I raise a flag of revolt against him? Should I imprison Antonia and Titus? Should I create anarchy by inciting people against the King? Should I defy the King and invade the Greek territory? [*He takes out the sword from its sheath.*] The gods of the sky may bear witness that Pushyamitr can color the Gangaa water red with the blood of the Greeks. [*to Patanjali*] Gurudev!

[*Patanjali does not respond.*]

Gurudev*!* [*in a cool, determined voice*] I have heard the clarion call of the motherland. Kindly bless me.

[*Patanjali opens his eyes and blesses him with raised right hand*]

Patanjali: "*Yogah karmasu kaushalam.*" Yoga is dexterity in action. You must find a new path.

[*He closes his eyes in meditation again.*]

[*Pushyamitr kneels and bows.*]

[SCENE FADES OUT]

'ONCE IN INDIA': Scenes from an earlier production in India

Scene 15

CHARACTERS

Antonia ‖ Titus ‖ Heliodorus ‖ Pushyamitr ‖ Brihadrath
Prajaamukh 1 ‖ Prajaamukh 2

[The Royal Court. The Greek bodyguard Heliodorus is standing behind the throne kept in the center. Antonia is standing nearby to welcome the Courtiers. Titus enters.]

Antonia: *Bhante*! [*She goes to Titus, holds him by his arm, and takes him to the front of the stage.*] Titus, I hope everything is well.

Titus: Don't worry. I have managed the two People's Representatives, the honorable Prajamukhs. They will only say what we want them to.

Antonia: [*pleased*] Good! You managed! How did you manage?

Titus: The way they get managed. Just throw a few gold coins before them. These Indians get sold very cheaply.

Antonia: Has the army chief refused to be sold? Why could you not purchase him?

Titus: He is the only one who has escaped our net. Don't worry. Titus will not give up easily.
[*Two Prajamukhs enter.*]

Antonia: [*receives them with folded hands and then looking at Titus*] Kindly get them seated. I am going to request *Mahaaraaj* to come in.

Titus: Respected Prajamukhs, kindly come. Where's the third Prajaamukh?

Prajaamukh 1: He is unwell. I met him in the morning. Otherwise, who would not come running at the *Mahaaraaj's* invitation?

Prajaamukh 2: *Bhante*, you also invited us. We had to come.

Titus: The Minister Veersen hasn't come?

Veersen: [*entering*] I have also come, *Dharm-mahaamaatra*. [*flatteringly*] Just as the King is a devotee of yours, I am also your devotee. We will advise whatever you want. Am I not correct, *Bhante*?

Titus: No Minister, you are not correct. We are all bound by *dharma*—the truth. Our advice will also be *dharma*-based. [*suddenly looking at the door*] *Senaapati* has arrived.
[*Pushyamitr enters. Titus gestures to Heliodorus.*]

Heliodorus: [*requesting*] *Senaapati* Sir! Kindly stop.
[*Pushyamitr stops at the gate. Heliodorus goes near him.*]
Sir, today weapons are prohibited inside the court chamber.

Pushyamitr: They are prohibited but not for the army chief. You are a new bodyguard. A Greek. You are not aware of the State protocol. Carrying arms inside the court chamber is *Senaapati's* prerogative.

Heliodorus: Sir, this is true. But for today, there are special orders.

Pushyamitr: [*annoyed*] Whose?

Heliodorus: Those of the King himself. Today's meeting is extraordinary. Today, even *Senaapati* won't carry arms to it.

Pushyamitr: [*concealing his annoyance*] It is my duty to obey the King's commands. [*He hands his arms over to Heliodorus.*]
[*Heliodorus exits with the weapons in hand.*]

Titus: *Senaapati* Pushyamitr Shung, kindly take your seat.
[*Pushyamitr enters. The Prajamukhs and*

Ministers greet him with folded hands. Pushyamitr takes his seat. Heliodorus enters.]

Heliodorus: Attention! Maurya King, *Mahaaraaj* Brihadrath is arriving.
[Brihadrath and Antonia enter. All the Courtiers stand up. Brihadrath goes to the two Prajamukhs and greets them with folded hands, sits on the throne and then gestures the Courtiers to sit down.]

Brihadrath: Today I have specially invited the Prajamukhs for their advice. I welcome them.
[*He gestures to Antonia to conduct the Court's proceedings.*]

Antonia: The glory of our King has spread all over the world. He is a renunciate at heart. He is on the throne of Paataliputr for the welfare of all living beings. In a few days, he will go on retreat to the Buddhist monastery for four months. During those months, he will not speak to or meet anyone. He will only meditate.

Brihadrath: In my absence, Prime Minister Aaryaa Antonia will look after the affairs of the State. She insists that I should only retreat after making decisions on some crucial matters. I need to consult you on these matters. Prime Minister, you may place the matter up for discussion before the august assembly.

Antonia: Salutations at the lotus feet of our beloved *Mahaaraaj.* Honorable Courtiers, everyone knows that the Magadh empire has no enemies anywhere in the world. Our King's message of love and compassion has reached all, even those in far-away countries.

Veersen: How true!

Antonia: An army is needed to defend against enemies. Since we do not have enemies, we do not need to defend against anyone. So what is the use of having an army?

Veersen: You are right, Prime Minister.

Antonia: *Bhante* Aananda has proposed that the army may be dismantled, and that the money we spent on it be used for the welfare of mankind.

Brihadrath: Does anyone want to speak about the proposal?

Pushyamitr: *Mahaaraaj*, I would like to say something.

Brihadrath: Yes, *Senaapati*. Go ahead.

Pushyamitr: In international politics, friends and foes keep changing. Today's friend may become an enemy tomorrow. We cannot risk tomorrow's security today.

Titus: We have to change this thinking. The very moment we think that our friend can become our foe tomorrow, a seed of doubt against our friend is sown. This doubt is what turns him into our enemy. [*emphatically*] *Senaapati*, we have to change our thinking.

Brihadrath: *Bhante*, you have spoken very rightly. If we see the world with the eyes of a friend, we will only find friends all around us. And if we look for enemies, we will only find enemies.

Titus: What a profound statement!

Pushyamitr: So the enemy who set fire to the Zeus temple was of your own creation?

Antonia: [*defending Titus*] We are speaking on a philosophical level—not about the Zeus temple.

Brihadrath: *Senaapati* Pushyamitr, your heart is full of violence. This is natural. After all, you are a soldier! To realize the power of non-violence, you will have to emerge from the limitations of violence.

Antonia: King Ashok did conquer Kaling, but to win their hearts, he had to have recourse to non-violence.

Pushyamitr: Yet King Ashok never dismantled his army.

Antonia: If non-violence is in our hearts, it would automatically resonate in the hearts of our enemies.

Pushyamitr: If the Greek King Minender invades us, what will we do?

Titus: He will not attack us.

Pushyamitr: Shall we welcome him with open arms?

Titus: Why would the Greeks attack us? They are our friends. They are devoted to our King. They want to install a life-size statue of our King in their cities of Gaandhaar and Bactria.

Antonia: Even powerful armies surrender before the strength of non-violence.

Titus: If an invader comes to kill us, but then sees love for him in our eyes, how could he raise his hands to kill us?

Pushyamitr: *Mahaaraaj*, if such a large army is dismantled, there would be great disaffection. No food would be cooked in thousands of homes. How would their families survive?

Brihadrath: Alright. I have listened to you. The Prajamukhs will keep in mind *Senaapati's* objections while giving their considered opinion.

Antonia: After retrenchment, soldiers will have plenty of work to do. Thousands of acres of land are lying barren. The ex-soldiers can make it cultivable. They can grow food for the poor countries of the world.

Brihadrath: In Prayaag City, there is going to be a Kumbh fair. Tens of thousands of people will gather there to bathe in holy rivers. Ex-soldiers can

look after law and order, sweep the roads and clean the toilets too.
[*Nobody responds.*]

Brihadrath: Our Minister Veersen is very quiet. What does he think?

Veersen: *Mahaaraaj*! *Senaapati* is right. If the entire army is dismantled, there may be chaos and anarchy. It is also possible that soldiers may revolt and indulge in looting and violence.

Brihadrath: Should the army not be dismissed?

Veersen: It will not be prudent to dismantle the entire army in one go. In the first instance, one-fourth of the army can be dismissed. Later on, the remaining soldiers can be dismissed—in various instalments.

Pushyamitr: [*to Veersen*] I suggest that after the dismissal of one-fourth of the army, the remaining soldiers should be equipped with new weapons.

Titus: When the entire army is to be dismissed one day, why should we waste money on its new weaponry? It will continue to manage in the future, the way it has managed with its old weapons until now.

Veersen: *Dharm-mahaamaatra's* suggestion is valid.

Brihadrath: Honored Prajamukhs! You have listened to the proposal of the Prime Minister and *Dharm-mahaamaatra*. You have also listened to the

army chief's objections thereon. You are the representatives of our people. You are the voice of our subjects. We are awaiting your advice.
[*Both Prajamukhs consult each other in whispers, then Prajaamukh1 stands up.*]

Prajaamukh 1: My salutations at the divine feet of King Brihadrath.
[*Brihadrath blesses him by raising his right hand.*]
I have listened very carefully to the proposals of the Prime Minister and *Dharm-mahaamaatra*. I also considered the *Senaapati's* objections. We Prajamukhs are unanimous in our opinion that the Magadh empire has no enemies, and therefore does not need an army to defend it. Hence, the army can be dismantled. But due to the consideration of law and order, only one-fourth of the army may be retrenched now, and the rest in due course.

Prajaamukh 1: [*standing*] Supreme Lord! *Mahaaraaj*! Our considered opinion is that there is also no need to re-equip the remaining army with new weapons.

Prajaamukh 2: [*standing up*] Your Great Lustrous Highness, the army does not have any work during times of peace. It should engage in clearing the forests, making the barren land cultivable and then growing food on it. It should also undertake city sanitation, sweeping the streets and cleaning the toilets. [*They sit down.*]

Pushyamitr: *Mahaaraaj,* we are here only to serve our people. I have maximum respect for the voice

of the people. I bow to the two representatives of our people. I am in agreement with them. I withdraw all of my objections. Now the decision of the King, who loves his subjects as a father loves his children, will be a command for me.
[*All are taken aback by Pushyamitr's U-turn, but nobody speaks.*]

Brihadrath: [*looking up, as though talking to God*] Lord Buddha said that this life is full of suffering. Man increases this suffering in his life by his acts of violence. If we want to get rid of suffering in life, we will have to take refuge in non-violence. [*He stands up.*] Non-violence is the absolute religion. It cannot be defeated. The power of non-violence is unconquerable. There is no enemy of non-violence. It never fails. It is the ornament of the brave. Dying in non-violence is bravery. Dying in violence is cowardice. Powerful armies cannot stand before the might of non-violence.

Titus: What a great truth!

Brihadrath: If the Greek King invades to take possession of our land, villages, cities, and riches, we will not resist. We will hand over to him our land, villages, cities, and riches ourselves. It will put the Greek King to shame. He will give everything back to us. Non-violence conquers hearts. It changes the heart. If a killer enters our country with a naked sword in his hand, we will not resist him. We will face the violence with non-violence. If he kills us, we will get killed. By dying in non-violence, we will become immortal.

Titus: Such a noble statement.

Brihadrath: [*sitting on the throne*] We agree with the Prajamukhs' advice. One-fourth of the army will be retrenched. The rest of the army will do social work. On the night of the next full moon, I will go into retreat at the Ashokaaraam Monastery for four months. Prime Minister Antonia will carry on the State affairs in my absence.

Pushyamitr: *Mahaaraaj*, I want to make a submission. The soldiers would like to seek the blessings of their beloved King, for the last time, on that great day of their retrenchment. As their first step towards non-violence, they will surrender their arms in your divine presence.
[*Brihadrath looks towards Antonia for advice. She nods in affirmation.*]

Antonia: *Senaapati's* request is acceptable.

Brihadrath: [*raising his right hand in blessing*] So be it.
[*He sits cross-legged, closes his eyes and goes into meditation.*]
[*Antonia gestures everyone to leave. Veersen and the two Prajamukhs come to Antonia and bow with folded hands before leaving. Titus moves to stand near Antonia.*]
[*While exiting, Pushyamitr suddenly returns to Antonia.*]

Pushyamitr: I had come determined not to let the army dismantle, but...

Antonia: But what?

Pushyamitr: There was something divine in the *Mahaaraaj's* voice that transformed me. I was completely mesmerized. It appeared to me as if the person sitting before me was a celestial being; a god descended from the skies! I was blinded by the rays emanating from his halo. My heart said to me, "Pushyamitr, are you blind? Can't you recognize this divine being?" And I surrendered to him.

Titus: At last wisdom has dawned upon you. *Tathaagat* protects those who seek refuge in Him.

Pushyamitr: Both of you should be emulated for your devotion to *Mahaaraaj*. I bow before you both. [*He bows before Antonia and Titus with folded hands. The two exchange sly smiles.*]

[SCENE FADES OUT]

Scene 16

CHARACTERS

Pushyamitr ‖ Soldier 1 ‖ Soldier 2 ‖ Soldier 3 ‖ Soldier 4

[The lonely corner of a forest at night. Pushyamitr enters with a flaming torch in his hand. He claps thrice. Four soldiers come out of hiding to join him. One of the soldiers takes the torch from the army chief's hand.]

Pushyamitr: You have come! What is the news?

Soldier 1: Ever since the soldiers heard the news of the army dismantling, they have been simmering with anger and despondence.

Soldier 2: We are sword-wielders, not broom-wielders. We will commit suicide before cleaning the public toilets.

Soldier 3: Antonia and the monk will commit suicide, not us. We know how to kill. We have only learned how to cut a head with one stroke of a sword.

Soldier 4: This is the Greeks' conspiracy; they want to take possession of the country by any means, fair or foul.

Soldier 3: They have already taken possession of the country. After the *Mahaaraaj's* retreat to the monastery, Antonia will rule over us.

Soldier 1: *Mahaaraaj* is a noble soul. He is unable to understand these peoples' cunningness.

Soldier 4: He understands everything. But he is helpless. He is infatuated with Antonia.

Soldier 2: She is a *Vishkanyaa,* a poison girl sent to destroy the Indian King and India. We will suck her poison and her blood too.

Pushyamitr: There is no use for blind fury. We have to decide what should be done. What does the army want?

Soldier 3: They want to revolt. They want to set fire to the Royal Palace.

Pushyamitr: [*probing*] Only the Royal Palace?

Soldier 3: [*stammering*] Yes, only the Palace.

Pushyamitr: My spies inform me that some soldiers wanted to arson my camp too.
[*Soldier 3 does not reply.*]

Pushyamitr: Why are you quiet? Answer. Your *Senaapati* assures you that no action will be taken against any one of you. I only want to know the truth.

Soldier 3: *Senaapati*, only a few soldiers...

Pushyamitr: Were you leading the group of those soldiers, Malay-Ketu?
[*Soldier 3 does not reply.*]
Answer me.

Soldier 3: *Senaapati*, that was momentary. Excuse us.

Pushyamitr: You four are my trusted disciples. You are fierce warriors. You are my strength. You are my arms...and I lost your confidence!

Soldier 3: *Senaapati*, kindly forgive us.

Pushyamitr: The Greek King Minender can attack us any time. Thousands of Greeks who have settled here during the last hundred years are Minender's spies. As soon as the army is dismantled or the army revolts, the Greeks will invade India.

Soldier 1: We know this, *Senaapati*!

Pushyamitr: This is the decisive moment. Today, history will be written; whether Indians can keep their freedom intact, or will they lose it to the Greeks. The responsibility to make history lies with *Senaapati* and his four valiant soldiers.

Soldier 4: Kindly excuse us. We received news that you have entered into a deal. You have surrendered to the Greeks—Antonia and the monk. You supported the dismantling of the army.

Pushyamitr: [*shocked*] Entered into a deal! The *Senaapati* entered into a deal with the aliens? Sold off his motherland? Beytrayed his countrymen?
[*No one responds.*]
Why don't you reply? Why are you quiet? Your *Senaapati* is a traitor? The punishment for betraying the country is death. It is your duty to punish the traitor with death. I give you my sword. [*He hands over his sword to Soldier 4.*] Mangal Sen, finish the life of the traitor.
[*Soldier 4 hesitates for some time, then musters the courage to place his sword against Pushyamitr's chest.*]
What are you waiting for? Put the sword into my chest.

Soldier 4: [*abruptly*] I cannot do it.

Pushyamitr: Why not? Can't you even do this much! It is your duty to punish the enemy of your country.

Soldier 4: You are not the enemy of the country.

Pushyamitr: Mangal Sen, emotion has overcome you. Your soft corner for your Guru has been aroused. Alright, give the sword to your companion. You finish the life of the betrayer of the motherland. This is my command.
[*Mangal Sen hesitatingly holds the sword with trembling hands for some time, and then passes it to Soldier 1, who hands it over to Soldier 2.*]

Soldier 2: *Senaapati*, I beg your pardon.

Pushyamitr: Would you not punish the enemy of your country?

Soldier 2: You are not the enemy of our country. I have looked into your eyes. A voice inside tells me that you are not the betrayer of the motherland. [*He kneels down and places the sword at Pushyamitr's feet.*]
[*Other soldiers also kneel down with bowed heads at Pushyamitr's feet.*]

Pushyamitr: Get up. My brave soldiers, get up. Bravery is not enough. One also has to devise strategy in war. Get up, my brave hearts.
[*The Soldiers stand up.*]

Pushyamitr: [*picking up the sword*] Let us put our hands onto this sword and swear that destruction of the enemies of our motherland is the only reason for us to be alive.

ALL: [*putting their hands onto the sword*] Destruction of the enemies of our motherland is the only reason for us to be alive.

[SCENE FADES OUT]

Scene 17

CHARACTERS

Antonia ‖ Titus ‖ Pushyamitr ‖ Prajaamukh 1 ‖ Prajaamukh 2 ‖ Heliodorus ‖ Veersen ‖ Umbrella-Bearer ‖ A Number of Dancers, Drum-Beaters, Conch-Blowers, Courtiers, Etc.

[The blue light on the cyclorama makes it to look like a vast blue sky. Near it is a parapet or barricade (about 3-4 feet high) to give the effect that the scene is being enacted on a raised platform or terrace. The impression is to be given to the audience that beyond the barricade, and below the stage, thousands of soldiers are standing, ready to surrender their arms before the King.

Near the barricade, on one side of the stage, Heliodorus is standing with a lance. Antonia and Titus are in conversation on the stage near the audience.]

Antonia: Today is a very auspicious day. Today, one-fourth of the army will be dismantled.

Titus: And from today onwards, Antonia will be the sovereign Head of the empire.

Antonia: Only for four months…It is also possible that the King may never return from his retreat. Anything can happen! [*smiling mysteriously*] Yes, anything can happen!
[*Senaapati Pushyamitr enters.*]

Pushyamitr: [*to Titus*] *Bhante,* the soldiers are getting impatient to catch a glimpse of *Mahaaraaj* before being relieved from the army service.

Antonia: The fear was that the army may revolt.

Titus: How could they have revolted? Ever since King Ashok's times, our people have been aware of the teachings of *Dhamma*, *Sangh* and non-violence. They know the power of non-violence.

Pushyamitr: The soldiers will behold the King, and be blessed. Thereafter, on behalf of all the soldiers, I will surrender my sword at the feet of the King. After that, all the soldiers will place their swords on the ground in front of them and be relieved from the army.
[*The cries 'Long live King Brihadrath' and 'Victory to King Brihadrath' are heard from below the ground.*]

Pushyamitr: [*excited*] Soldiers are chanting slogans in honor of our King. [*He runs to the barricade and waves to the soldiers.*]

Titus: What a golden coincidence! Today, the King is going for a retreat in the monastery, and today, soldiers, inspired by non-violence are surrendering their arms.

[*Both Titus and Antonia go near Pushyamitr.*]

Pushyamitr: [*addressing the soldiers standing below*] Soldiers! I am your *Senaapati* Pushyamitr Shung... Have patience. Keep quiet. After a little while, our most respected, revered, god-like King, the King of Kings, the Sun of Maurya dynasty, *Mahaaraaj* Brihadrath will be here to bless you. Here on this royal platform are the Prime Minister Aaryaa Antonia and *Dharm-mahaamaatra* Aananda. They are also blessing you.

[*Antonia and Titus wave to the soldiers. The soldiers' victory chants are heard.*]

Pushyamitr: Soldiers, you are fortunate because today, after leaving the army, you are going to be non-violent soldiers. From now onwards, you will never kill anybody, but only get killed. Our King has taught us that powerful armies are ineffective before the might of non-violence. [*Victory chants are heard off-stage, while he comes to the front right corner of the stage.*] Thousands of years ago, the demon Raavan had abducted the goddess Seetaa. Lord Raam avenged this national shame by killing him. He was not aware of the effectiveness of non-violence, and therefore took recourse to violence. [*He moves to the front center of the stage.*] When Arjun refused to fight in the middle of war, Lord Krishna called him a coward. Lord Krishna was ignorant of the potency of non-violence. [*Victory slogans are heard off-stage, while he moves to the front left corner of the stage.*] If the Greeks come to invade us from the Northwest, *Bhante* will go to confront them with a group of monks. The Greeks will be vanquished by the monks' non-violent power. [*He moves down stage centre.*] If the Greeks come with naked swords, we will stretch our necks out to be killed. Even in our death, we will not hate them. Our hearts will always remain filled with love for them. With non-violence, even in death, we will become immortal.

[*The loud sound of a number of conch-shells blowing is heard from off-stage, followed by the deafening sounds of beating drums and other musical instruments. Dancers enter, followed by the King and a procession of people—bodyguards, courtiers, musicians, instrumentalists, and the umbrella-bearer holding the umbrella over the King's head. Brihadrath takes a round on the stage, acknowledging the greetings of the people all around him. He goes to the back of the stage, near the barricade, and waves to the soldiers below. Pushyamitr shows a garland of flowers to the soldiers below, and then formally garlands the King, as though on behalf of the soldiers below. Pushyamitr shows a sword to the soldiers below, and bows formally before the King with the sword in both of his hands. The King bows to take the sword, but Pushyamitr stabs him. All the music suddenly stops. There is absolute silence for some time.*]

Brihadrath: Pushyamitr, you...? [*He staggers a few steps and falls down.*]

[*Titus takes out a dagger concealed in his clothes but a soldier puts a sword into his back. Titus lets the dagger fall from his hand. At the same time, Antonia and Heliodorus are overpowered by the soldiers. The scene freezes. Pushyamitr goes to the front of the stage. He is seen in a spotlight. All other lights on the stage are gradually put out.*]

Pushyamitr: Motherland! Whenever an alien invader casts his greedy eyes on you, there will always be a Pushyamitr to sacrifice him on the altar of your holy feet. [*He holds the sword by its handle and solemnly touches his forehead with its upright blade, as a sign of reverance.*]

[*Pushyamitr's words echo in the auditorium.*]

CURTAIN

THE KING OF MATHURAA

Translated from Hindi by
Vijaya Agrawal

THE KING OF MATHURAA

SYNOPSIS

The King of Mathuraa is the reinterpretation of a well-known Indian mythological tale, in contemporary theatrical idiom. King Kans of Mathuraa has been portrayed as a dictator, who is no different from modern-day dictators like Hitler, Stalin, or China's Mao Tse-tung, etc. Thus, King Kans' story is the story of all the dictators who have appeared on the world stage, from time to time, in different countries. In effect, the play is a clinical analysis of the phenomena of dictatorship.

The Mythology

Once upon a time, there was a King of Mathuraa named Ugrasen, who belonged to the Yaadav clan. He had a son named Kans, who was married to Princess Asti, the daughter of King Jaraasandh of Magadh. King Ugrasen arranged the marriage of his daughter Devakee with Vasudev, a scion of the rulers of Hastinaapur. After the marriage ceremonies were over, Kans heard a voice from the sky that the eighth son of the new couple would kill him. Fearing for his life, Kans dethroned his father Ugrasen and put him in jail. He also imprisoned the newly married couple and anointed himself as the King of Mathuraa. He ordered that all the children born to his sister Devakee and her husband Vasudev be killed.

Although the voice from the sky had warned that their eighth son would kill him, he did not want to take any chances. He ordered that all the children born to Devakee and Vasudev be killed. Accordingly, Kans killed seven newborn babies of the couple. But when the eighth son was born to them, he was miraculously exchanged, as if by divine ordination, with a newborn daughter of a village chief named Nand. When the eighth newborn baby girl was brought before Kans, he was surprised that the baby was not a boy, as was predicted. He still did not want to take any chances. He killed the girl by beating her against the stony floor. After her death, the girl reappeared as a goddess in a blaze of light in the sky, and declared that Kans' killer had been born and was being brought up elsewhere.

Kans assigned the demon Pootnaa the task of killing all children born during this period by smearing her nipples with poison and putting them into children's mouths. But, miraculously again, a child named Krishna, the eighth son of Devakee and Vasudev, whom the village chief Nand was raising, did not die. Instead, Krishna suckled Pootnaa to death.

Krishna grew up into a charming, handsome, flute-playing adolescent. All attempts made by the vile King Kans to kill him failed. At last, Kans planned to kill Krishna by trickery. He organized a wrestling match in which Krishna was made to fight with carefully selected royal wrestlers. But a miracle happened again. King Kans himself watched as Krishna defeated the royal wrestler in the public match. After defeating him, Krishna climbed onto the royal platform and killed Kans. The public cheered Krishna on because everyone hated Kans for his ruthless, autocratic dictatorship.

Krishna is hailed by Hindus as a reincarnation of God, who came to destroy evil on earth.

The Play

The King of Mathuraa is based on Indian mythology. It creatively reinterprets the story of the wild and wicked King Kans as that of a modern dictator for contemporary audiences. Through Kans, the play attempts to identify and portray all the *Kansaas* (dictators) who have appeared throughout history in various countries.

The play starts at a point where Kans has become an all-powerful dictator. He has decimated all opposition to his tyrannical rule and is reigning supreme. Looking back on his life's journey, from being an ordinary music-loving youth to a mighty autocrat, worshipped like a god by terrified, subdued masses, Kans realizes he has lost all those who were with him at the commencement of his journey. Friends, companions, beloved, wife—all have been left behind. Now at the pinnacle of his power, he is alone, and frightened. Afraid for his life, he is unable to sleep. He *"roams about restlessly, alone in the dark of the night, like a ghost, from one turret to another, from one parapet of the fort to another, in the vain hope that from sheer exhaustion, he may fall asleep, even if only for a moment."*

Alone and lonely, Kans looks back at the road he has traversed. Memories start crowding his mind in the form of flashbacks in the play. When anyone thinks of their past, it is not likely that they would recall past events and people in chronological order. Depending upon their relative importance, it is possible that older memories may be recalled earlier and more recent memories come later. Accordingly, the flashbacks do not adhere to the timeline and appear as per the demand of the play. The play adheres to its mythology in all its essentials. The miraculous events have been rationalized. Pootnaa, the demon associate of King Kans, has been portrayed as a village belle and Kans' beloved, whom Kans ultimately sacrificed at the altar of his all-consuming ambition.

GEOGRAPHY

Mathuraa: The name of a city located about 200 miles southwest of Delhi, ruled by the Yaadav clan and sandwiched between two mighty empires of Magadh in the East and Hastinaapur in the Northwest.

Magadh: The name of a Kingdom with its capital at Pataaliputra (present day Patna), ruled by King Jaraasandh. King Jaraasandh's daughter Asti was married to King Kans of Mathuraa. To ward off the influence of Hastinaapur on the Kingdom of Mathuraa, King Jaraasandh sent two army generals named Baahuk and Vritighn to Mathuraa, along with a group of soldiers.

Hastinaapur: The name of the capital of the Kingdom of the Kaurav clan, located near Delhi. They also wanted to bring Mathuraa under their influence, and thus were rivals of the Magadh King Jaraasandh.

GLOSSARY

Aarati: A ritual of worshipping/paying respect to gods or individuals by moving a small lighted lamp (lighted cotton wick soaked in purified butter) in a clockwise, circular motion in front of the idol of a god or the face of an individual.

Ascetic: An individual who withdraws from the world and devotes his or her entire life to the service of God and society.

Ashvamedha Yagn: A ritual performed by any powerful king who wanted to assert his sovereignty over neighboring kings. In this ritual, a horse was led into the neighboring kingdoms, followed by an army. If the armies of the neighboring kings did not capture the horse, this would imply their submission to the king performing the *yagna*. But if they captured the horse, they would have to fight the king's army. If the king performing the *yagna* lost the battle, the *yagna* would fail.

Devee: Literally meaning "goddess" in Hindi and Sanskrit. It is also used as an honorific prefix before the names of women.

Gokul: Name of the village where Lord Krishna was raised. As per mythology, Krishna, born to Devakee and Vasudev, was miraculously moved to the household of Nand, who was chief of the Gokul village.

Himaalayaas: The mountain range that constitutes the northern border of India.

Indr: Mythological King of gods.

Jaraasandh: King of Magadh; father of queen Asti; father-in-law of Kans

Kaashee: A holy city and pilgrimage center of India.

Kanyaakumaree: The southernmost tip of the Indian peninsula.

Kaurav: The ruling dynasty of the Kingdom of Hastinaapur.

Kosee Village: A village in Mathuraa Kingdom.

Krishna: Believed by Hindus to be a reincarnation of God in a human body, to protect the noble and destroy the evil. Also called "Lord Krishna."

Lord Vishnu: Believed by Hindu mythology to be the sustaining force of a formless God, which has three aspects: Brahma (the creator), Vishnu (the sustainer) and Mahesh/Shiva (the destroyer).

Mahaaraaj: Literally meaning "Great King" in Hindi and Sanskrit; an honorific addressed to a king.

Nand: The chief of Gokul village; Krishna's foster father. As per Hindu mythology, Krishna, the eighth son of Devakee and Vasudev, was miraculously moved to Nand's household, where he was raised.

Narasingh Avataar: As per Hindu mythology, Lord Vishnu's reincarnation as half-man, half-lion, to kill the demon King Hiranyakashipu.

Pootnaa: A demon associate of Kans to whom he assigned the job of killing all the children born in the Mathuraa Kingdom, out of his fear of being killed by the eighth son born to his sister Devakee.

Raajgriha: Capital of Magadh .

Rati: The goddess of love; female Eros; the most beautiful woman.

Saawan: One of the months of the Hindu calendar.

Shiva Shanker: A Hindu god.

Shree: An honorific for men.

Vasudev: Husband of Kans' sister Devakee

Yaadav: A caste / clan name.

Yagn: Fire sacrifice.

CHARACTERS

Kans	The King of Mathuraa
Ugrasen	Father of Kans; former King of Mathuraa
Pralamb	Minister in the Mathuraa Kingdom
Pradyot	Army chief; childhood friend of King Kans
Baahuk	Army Commander of Magadh; loaned by the King of Magadh to Kans
Vritrighn	Army chief of the King of Magadh on special visit to Mathuraa
Asti	Queen of Mathuraa; Daughter of King of Magadh
Swaati	Beloved of Kans; a village belle
Devakee	Sister of Kans; wife of Vasudev; closely related to Hastinaapur Kingdom
Narrator	Character in the Performance Troupe
Two Assistants	Characters in the Performance Troupe
Hiranyakashipu	Character in the Performance Troupe
Prahlaad	Character in the Performance Troupe
Fisherman	
Guard	
Three Hangmen	

'THE KING OF MATHURAA ': Some scenes from an earlier production in India

Act One

[Two acting-spots are established by the stage setting. The first is the open terrace of a palace, where a royal chair is placed beside a stone pillar soaring high into the sky, with a huge gong and hammer nearby. The second is a clearing in the jungle by the side of a big tree.

When the curtain goes up, the stage is dimly lit, indicating that it is nightime. After a while, a small but sharp light beam hits the base of the stone pillar and gradually moves up to the top. It remains lit throughout the play, symbolizing Kans' soaring ambition. Kans enters, exhausted.]

Kans: How ironic! So many nights have passed longing for a wink of sleep. While the stupid commoners wrapped in their torn garments, with stones for pillows, sleep soundly on the bare ground, I, the Brightest of the Bright, Bravest of the Brave, Mighty King of Kings, the Highest Lord God Kans, roam about restlessly, alone in the dark of the night, like a ghost, from one turret to another, from one parapet of the fort to the other, in the vain hope that from sheer exhaustion I may fall asleep, even if only for a moment. All I want is simply some sleep. [*He sits down on his throne.*] Some sleep…sleep... [*He closes his eyes for a moment, but soon lets out a fearful scream. His hands try to free his neck from another pair of imaginary hands throttling him, and he slips from the throne to the floor. Just then, a Guard comes running in with a spear in hand.*]

Guard: Lord! Almighty God!

Kans: [*in a dream*] Help! Help!

Guard: Lord! [*louder*] My Lord!

Kans: [*opening his eyes*] Huh?

Guard: Were you dreaming? My Lord!

Kans: [*involuntarily*] Yes... [*regaining composure*] No. [*getting up*] Guard! What is it?

Guard: Was it a dream?

Kans: You may leave now.
[*The Guard kneels, bows, and then exits.*]

Kans: What a fearful dream! Two terrifying hands.

Thousands of men, women, aged, children and youth—thousands of faces, thousands of bodies, but hands, only two! Terrible, powerful, cruel, frightful hands, whose iron fingers were tightening around my neck as if to stop my breathing. [*He starts laughing aloud hysterically and mockingly.*] Afraid? Lord Kans! The Almighty God was frightened! He was terrified. [*His laughter turns into sobbing.*] The very thought of the sleep for which I have been craving makes me shake and shudder with fear. [*The sound of a flute comes from backstage. He is terror-stricken after hearing it.*] Again the same sound—notes of the flute; terrible, piercing the ears as if... [*He hastily sounds the gong.*]

[*The Guard re-enters and bows.*]

Guard: Almighty God!

Kans: I again heard the sound of a flute. It seems that the rebel youth leader Krishna is hiding somewhere in the palace itself. Tell the Army Chief, Pradyot, to capture him and bring him here.

Guard: Your order shall be obeyed. [*He bows and exits.*]

Kans: In sleep, the grip of the terrifying iron hands, and while awake, the tune of the flute heralding the arrival of death. What torture! No peace... in sleep or while awake! I'm already dead while alive. Sleeping and waking have become one. The line dividing life and death has blurred. Questions linger in this confusion. Is every tyranny self-torture? Every murder a suicide?

[*He comes to the forefront of the stage.*]
Where does this story begin? The story of an ordinary man's extraordinary ambition. The story of an everyday man becoming God. The story of warm blood flowing through a healthy, pulsating heart, hardening gradually into a stone; of dying, bit by bit, embracing death every moment, while still alive. Where does this story begin?

FLASHBACK I BEGINS

[*Ugrasen enters and approaches the child Kans.*]

Ugrasen: [*affectionately*] Kans!

Kans: Yes father, King of Kings.

Ugrasen: Which weapon do you like the best?

Kans: What Sir?

Ugrasen: A sword, bow and arrow, spear, thunderbolt, mace…which one?

Kans: [*thinking*] Hmm…

Ugrasen: Yes, which is your favorite?

Kans: [*innocently*] Flute.

Ugrasen: Flute?

Kans: Yes father, I like flute the best.

Ugrasen: [*laughing loudly*] What's this?! I am talking about a sword, bow and arrow and thunderbolt, not about a flute and ankle bells. [*contemptuously*] This son of mine is a woman disguised in the garb of a man. Woman! Female! [*He exits, laughing scornfully.*]

Flashback I Ends

Kans: When did I hear this laughter, full of mockery? Years ago…ages back. But I can never forget it. I still hear it…the same, full of mockery and scorn—insulting every fibre of my being…

FLASHBACK II BEGINS

[*Swaati enters.*]

Swaati: Why are you so lost in thought, Lord Prince?

Kans: Swaati?

Swaati: What worries you so much that you don't even acknowledge my presence?

Kans: Oh something.

Swaati: May God give all your worries to me and shower all His blessings upon you.

Kans: [*tenderly*] Swaati!

Swaati: You look even more handsome when rapt in thought.

Kans: I am handsome?

Swaati: Yes.

Kans: Very handsome?

Swaati: Very handsome.

Kans: Like a woman?

Swaati: [*playfully*] More than a woman.

Kans: [*becoming very serious*] Don't I look like a man?

Swaati: Who says you don't?

Kans: Am I not lacking in masculinity?

Swaati: [*mischievously*] Don't ask me that!

Kans: Am I a man?

Swaati: [*smiling*] Why are you asking me this?

Kans: Tell me. Tell me, Swaati. Am I not a man?

Swaati: I can't tell you.

Kans: You have to tell me. Answer. Am I not a man?

Swaati: If I tell you the truth, then....

Kans: Then what?
[*Swaati keeps smiling.*]

Kans: [*loudly supplicating*] Then what?

Swaati: Every woman in Mathuraa will fall in love with you. Brightness dulls in the presence of your handsome looks. In a crowd of men, you are the man.

Kans: Does violence define manliness? Do cruelty, callousness, killing, bloodshed and murder make a man?

Swaati: No...

Kans: Don't try to console me.

Swaati: I am telling you the truth.

Kans: If you are telling the truth, then is my father, King of Kings, Lord Ugrasen a liar? Are all the noblemen of Mathuraa liars? Even the doorkeeper of the palace knows the truth. Vasudev knows, too.

Swaati: They don't know the truth.

Kans: Do you think they would have laughed at me if they had not known? Would everyone, from the King to the guard have openly ridiculed me? Don't give me false assurances. I am aware of the reality.

Swaati: I swear…

Kans: [*not allowing her to continue*] Don't swear to lies. Their feet are of clay; they will be washed away with the first flood of truth. Kans has been a fool—a stupid fool.

Swaati: What's wrong with you?

Kans: A man is one who kills and takes joy in shedding blood. Unfeeling, cruel, barbarous, blind and deaf—such is a man. [*squirming in mental anguish*] Why can't I bear the suffering of others? Why am I filled with pity when seeing others in pain? Why do tears well up in my eyes when I see others suffer? Why am I so effeminate? Why am I so weak?

Swaati: This isn't weakness.

Kans: I have been like this since birth. I have always dreamt of a world without barbarity. Everyone...all would be equal. Man would have sympathy for his fellow men. There would be music from the flute, the companion of my solitude. There would be perfume and flowers.

Swaati: People do not understand you. You are great—way ahead of your time.

Kans: [*vehemently*] But I have to live in the present time. This ancient sky will witness that I am born of this age and I shall live in this age. I will snatch the smug smiles away from the faces of all the people who have dared to ridicule me. Only when the blood of penance drips from those lips twisted in derision, will my burning heart full of vengeance be consoled.

Swaati: Don't say such things. It scares me…

Kans: Nobles had assembled for an archery competition organised to entertain the powerful and brave Yaadavs. At the King's bidding, Vasudev aimed at the right eye of the goat from a hundred steps away. The arrow found its target. The goat, tied to a stake, jumped once and fell down. Its scream was lost in the deafening, barbarous applause of the brave Yaadav. Vasudev looked around, gloriously victorious. His breast swelled with pride. Prince Kans was then ordered to pierce the left eye of the goat from a hundred steps away, to prove his archery skills. I aimed at the goat's left eye. Silence, for a few still moments. Those still moments were so eloquent. The silence asked me what was I doing? The entreating, helpless gaze of that goat, with blood streaming out of its right eye! I imagined tears of blood rolling down his left eye too. Truly, I saw tears of blood in its left eye. Blood dripped out of it even before I sent the arrow flying. I thought,

"Am I not an animal myself, about to kill a nearly dead creature? What is this madness all about?" I removed the arrow from the bow. Hundreds of eyes stared at me. Thorns pricking me. I told the King that I just couldn't do it. 'I knew it'—the King said. There was such scorn and hatred in his tone. 'You wear bangles on your wrists and play the flute. These masculine games are not meant for effeminate men.' Insult, humiliation, mockery and scorn. [*suddenly angry*] Stupid, barbarous brutes...

Swaati: Kans!

Kans: Swaati, I can foresee Kans' destiny. It is as clear as daylight. [*a little crazily*] A heap of innumerable corpses—the old, the young, the women, the children, all like lifeless puppets, like the pile of countless dead goats. Terrible eddies of vultures flying in the sky. The eyeball of an innocent child plucked out of its socket by a vulture, the blood-smeared flesh of the fair breast of some young woman, a vulture pecking at the strong arm of some young person… rising from the earth, farther up, violent, greedy, hot, burning red flames of fire and sparks, embers flying and falling: chaos, noise, stampede, shrieking, wailing. This is Kans' destiny...[*suddenly*] I am going, Swaati.

Swaati: [*upset*] Where?

Kans: [*as if possessed*] My destiny is beckoning me [*He comes closer to Swaati and tenderly takes her in his arms.*] Swaati! [*after a moment, suddenly*] I should go. [*He leaves at once.*]

Swaati: [*calling*] Kans! Listen! [*following him*] Wait. Come back. Kans…please come back. [*She exits while pursuing him.*]

Flashback ii ends

[*Kans re-enters in the present.*]

Kans: [*entering*] How do I come back, Swaati? I myself have destroyed all the bridges leading the way back. Now I have gone so far, so far that I can't even contemplate coming back. This path is difficult, full of thorns and gravel; walking upon it, my feet have developed sores. The valor of first flush of youth and ambition of world conquest have drained out of me, along with the blood that seeps from them. All that is left is a lifeless, tired, dull, deflated and defeated Kans, on the pinnacle of his achievement—absolutely alone.

FLASHBACK III BEGINS

[*Baahuk, Pralamb and Pradyot enter.*]

Kans: You all wait. I shall bring my father here to give special audience to Baahuk, the special emissary of King Jarasandh, the ruler of Magadh . [*He exits.*]

Pralamb: To give special audience... [*laughs tauntingly*]

Baahuk: I don't like Mathuraa, Pralamb.

Pradyot: Why not?

Baahuk: If you could just see the royal city of Raajgriha, the capital of Magadh, you would not want to see any other city in the whole world.

Pradyot: Everyone loves one's motherland; it cannot be compared with any other country.

Baahuk: General Pradyot, a city is comprised of citizens. Yaadavs don't know the city ways—uncultured, rustic and completely stupid as they are...
[*Kans enters with King Ugrasen.*]

Kans: Baahuk, the Special Emissary of King Jaraasandh of Magadh has come to make an offering at the feet of the ruler of the Yaadav.
[*Baahuk kneels and with both hands motions as if to present a sword to Ugrasen. As the King bends to take it, Pradyot lays a naked sword across his back.*]

Pradyot: You are a prisoner.
[*Pralamb bursts into mocking laughter, and Pradyot places the sword across the King's chest.*]

Ugrasen: [*in a rage*] Kans!

Pralamb: Not Kans…say "King of Kings." The King of Mathuraa.

Baahuk: Victory to King Kans.
[*Ugrasen looks outside for help.*]

Baahuk: All of your bodyguards have been defeated and put to the sword by soldiers from Magadh.

Pralamb: The more intelligent amongst them are busy counting the gold…

Baahuk: [*completing the sentence*]…given by *Mahaaraaj* Jaraasandh. Vasudev has been held captive in prison.

Pralamb: His new bride, Devakee, is keeping him company.

Kans: You married Devakee to Vasudev to secure an alliance with the Kauravs of Hastinaapur, and planned to make Vasudev the King of Mathuraa, denying my rightful claim.

Baahuk: Stupid fool!

Kans: [*tauntingly*] Kans is a poet, fit only to wear bangles like a woman and play the flute. Effeminate and cowardly! The same Kans who soiled his clothes out of fear is today the arbiter of your fate, my father.
[*Ugrasen gazes on uncomprehendingly.*]
King, my father! I had sworn to myself that that smile of mockery would be washed off

your lips one day, and that an entreaty for forgiveness would take its place. That day has arrived. [*in a highly controlled voice*] King, my father! Ask my pardon.

[*Ugrasen stands stunned.*]

Did you not hear me? King, my father! Ask for pardon. Do not test my patience.

[*Ugrasen indicates with meaningless sounds and hand gestures that he has lost his ability to speak.*]

Pradyot: It seems like the King has lost his voice.

Kans: No!

[*Pralamb laughs tauntingly.*]

No, you cannot become mute. I want you to apologize.

[*Ugrasen indicates again, in the same manner, that he has become dumb.*]

Pralamb: The King has really lost his ability to speak.

Baahuk: How can anyone keep his tongue in his mouth in the presence of the King of Kings, mighty Kans, and before the great prowess of the Magadh soldiers?

Kans: Take him away. Throw him in prison. Have it declared in the Yaadav empire that King Ugrasen has committed suicide. But the King, my father, should remain alive. May the best doctor help him speak again, so that he may kneel before me, beg for his life and apologize—with the same voice he had ridiculed me with. Take him away.

[*Pralamb, Baahuk and Pradyot exit, taking King Ugrasen with them.*]

Kans: King, my father! What have you done? I have been waiting forever for the moment you would apologize. I have savored this moment so often in my imagination. To make this moment come true, I have burned in the fire of vengeance for so many sleepless nights.
[*He closes his eyes to attempt to overcome emotions.*]

Flashback iii ends

Kans: [*narrating*] I was about five or six years old at the time. My father, Ugrasen, took me to the forest with him. In the middle of the forest, he tied his horse near a lake and kept shooting arrows at birds and fish. It began to grow dark after sunset. Father was very happy. After enjoying a few cups of wine, he addressed me.

FLASHBACK IV BEGINS

[*Ugrasen enters with the child Kans.*]

Ugrasen: Kans, can you go back to the royal palace alone?

Child Kans: [*with innocent pride*] Yes.

Ugrasen: You know the way?

Child Kans: This path goes straight to Mathuraa. We came the same way.

Ugrasen: Brave boy! Alright, I am going. You come by yourself.

Child Kans: Alone! by myself?

Ugrasen: Will you feel afraid?

Child Kans: [*scared*] No.

Ugrasen: Brave boy! Yaadav are born brave. [*He exits.*]

Child Kans: [*narrating*] I stood there stupified. Father mounted his horse and rode off with his bodyguards.

[*Sounds of the horse retreating are heard. Child Kans walks on the pathway, frightened.*]

The beat of the hoofs penetrated deeper and deeper into me, generating fear. I was alone in that dense, dark forest. Absolutely alone. It was an awful, deadly forest. A man-eater—a looming lion or a dreadful bear—under every tree in the dark… I was shaking with fear in every fibre of my body. Listening to my heartbeat, partly dazed, I limped along the pathway to Mathuraa. After a short distance, my father suddenly appeared from behind a tree and stood before me.

[*Ugrasen enters. Child Kans runs and clings to him like a five-year-old.*]

Child Kans: My royal father!

Ugrasen: Why are you crying? Are you scared? [*Kans keeps crying and does not answer.*] Were you scared?

Child Kans: [*crying*] Yes. [*Ugrasen grabs Child Kans by the arm and roughly jerks him.*]

Ugrasen: I am ashamed of you. [*contemptuously*] How can the Prince of the Yaadav be so afraid?! [*Child Kans starts crying loudly.*] Now you demonstrate your valor with tears? Stop crying. [*Child Kans continues to cry.*] Stop crying. [*He slaps Child Kans across the face.*] Say that, in the future, you will never feel scared.

Child Kans: [*sobbing*] In the future, I will never feel scared.

Ugrasen: I am a brave Yaadav.

Child Kans: I am a brave Yaadav. [*While repeating this, he suddenly brings both of his thighs together.*]

Ugrasen: [*noticing*] What's going on? Did you soil your clothes?

Child Kans: [*stammering*] N…n…no.

Ugrasen: Wet clothes! [*He hits Kans with both hands.*] Idiot! Coward! You weak thing…[*He continues to beat Kans and then exits angrily.*]

Child Kans: [*weeping*] Forgive me, royal father! Please forgive me. I will never feel afraid. I will never feel afraid. I will never fear. I shall never wet my clothes. Never fear nor soil my clothes, never. I am a brave Yaadav. Brave Yaadav... [*He exits while still speaking.*]

Flashback iv ends

FLASHBACK V BEGINS

[*Pralamb enters while speaking, as if addressing a public gathering.*]

Pralamb: The brave Yaadav, King Kans, is your protector. King Ugrasen wanted to make Vasudev the ruler of the Yaadav.

Pradyot: [*entering*] Vasudev is the enemy of Yaadavs. Vasudev's sister Kunti is married to the King of Hastinaapur. Vasudev wants to sell Mathuraa to Hastinaapur.

Pralamb: The weak Yaadav Republic, built with popular support from the Yaadav people, could not have survived in the face of an invasion.

Pradyot: That is why King Kans has dissolved the Yaadav Assembly and assumed all power.

Pralamb: Like his father-in-law, mighty King Jaraasandh of Magadh, he wants his land to become sovereign and to build a powerful Yaadav nation by uniting various Yaadav clans.

Baahuk: [*entering*] The Yaadav are in danger today. Your boundaries are not secure. At King Kans' invitation, Magadh soldiers have come to protect you. Magadh soldiers will lay down their lives for the Yaadav people.

Pralamb: King Kans shall fly the glorious Yaadav flag from the Himaalayaas to Kanyaakumaree.

Pradyot: Glory be to the Yaadav's valor.

Pralamb: King Kans shall destroy the forces of Hastinaapur that have mobilized at the borders, ready to attack us.

Pradyot: Glory be to King Kans.

Pralamb: Soldiers from Magadh are our friends.

Pradyot: King Jaraasandh of Magadh is our friend. [*Pralamb, Pradyot and Baahuk come forward on the stage, one by one, as if programmed like puppets to parrot slogans before gatherings of people in praise of the King.*]

Pralamb: Vasudev is a traitor.

Baahuk: Yaadav are in danger.

Pradyot: Glory be to King Kans.

[*All three continue to raise slogans mechanically, one by one, with raised fists.*]

Pralamb: Vasudev is a traitor.

Baahuk: Yaadav are in danger.

Pradyot: Glory be to King Kans.

[*Their voices die down gradually, but they continue to gesticulate like puppets as though they are still speaking.*]

[*Kans enters. He sounds the gong. All three freeze in their respective places.*]

[*The Guard enters. Pralamb, Pradyot and Baahuk line up at the rear of the stage with their backs towards the audience.*]

[*The Guard bows.*]

Guard: My Lord Almighty!

Kans: Where is the Minister Pralamb? Call him.

Guard: My Lord God! [*He bows and exits.*]

[*Pralamb comes to Kans and bows before him.*]

Kans: What's the news?

Pralamb: My Lord! The Yaadav are highly displeased. Their sympathies are with King Ugrasen, with Vasudev and Devakee. The Yaadav love their freedom. They are accustomed to freedom. They are finding having a despot intolerable.

[*Pradyot runs to Kans in panic and bows.*]

Pradyot: Lots of Yaadav have gathered outside the palace shouting slogans.
[*Baahuk comes to Kans with arrogant confidence.*]

Baahuk: The Magadh soldiers have routed them, like rays of the sun dispelling the mist. There is complete peace and order.

Pralamb: [*bowing*] Glory be to King Kans.

Pradyot: The cruel Yaadav have butchered two Magadh Soldiers.

Pralamb: [*bowing*] Glory be to King Kans.

Pradyot: The rebels have set fire to some of the soldiers' camps.

Baahuk: The rebels have been arrested and hanged in the city square. There is peace and order.

Pradyot: The Yaada*v* of Kosi village have refused to give revenue.

Baahuk: Kosee village and its inhabitants have been removed from the Yaadav Kingdom. Last night, the village was burnt. The fleeing inhabitants of the burning houses could not escape the soldiers surrounding the village. There is peace and order.

Pralamb: [*bowing*] Glory be to our Great King.

[*Queen Asti enters.*]

Kans: Asti!

Asti: King of Kings Kans! [*She bows.*]

Kans: Queen Asti! Welcome to the Princess of Magadh and the Queen of Mathuraa. [*Pralamb, Pradyot and Baahuk kneel and bow.*]

Asti: After hearing that you were surrounded by rebels, I could not sit back in Raajgriha.

Kans: But…

Asti: I am not alone. I've brought along the remaining soldiers as part of my dowry.

Kans: This is Pralamb, my Minister. This is Pradyot, our trusted army chief. It is his responsibility to look after the security of the royal palace and the ruler of Mathuraa. And, of course, you know the Magadh army chief Baahuk...

Asti: I'm delighted that you have brought your aides along with you. [*She moves a short distance away.*] Kans!
[*Kans goes near her.*]
These servants are enough to take care of the rebels. Don't waste your life on these trifles. Come closer. [*She lays her head on Kans' shoulder.*] I am waiting. [*looking at Kans' hand*] This flute of my body is eager to

burst into a seven-hued melody at the touch of your fingers. [*She starts spinning around where she stands, holding Kans and making him move around her.*] Come, let's drink wine from the cup of the moon, make love in this moonlight and touch the sky, swinging in passion... [*She continues to rotate.*]

[*Pralamb, Pradyot and Baahuk get up grasping each other's hands and revolve around Kans and Asti in the opposite direction. Their speed gradually increases as they sing a lullaby.* "The King may sleep We sing a lullaby"]

[*The volume of their singing starts in whispers and increases with the speed of their circling. At the climax, Kans lets out a scream. 'No—No!' He comes out and breaks the circle as others stand, motionless.*]

Kans: How can one sleep? Despite these helpers and assurances, there is fear—fear without a beginning—invisible, like a layer upon another layer, drop by drop, an ever-growing fear moving through the veins. [*thinking*] What has the astrologer predicted? What has he? [*screaming impulsively*] Why don't you reply? What did the astrologer say?

[*Baahuk, Pradyot and Pralamb stand behind Kans like marionettes.*]

All Three: [*repeating like parrots*] The eighth son of Vasudev and Devakee will destroy Kans.

Asti: [*laughs sneeringly*] The astrologer! The

Yaadav rebellion has petered out. It has been quelled. That is why people feel compelled to believe the absurd talk of an astrologer. It is like drowning the present in the wine of the future, even for a little while. [*She laughs loudly, sits on Kans' throne and then motions to Kans.*] Come here.
[*Kans goes closer to Asti, sits by her feet and places his head in her lap.*]
Sleep, Kans. Go to sleep. Don't worry. Baahuk, Pralamb and Pradyot are singing you a lullaby. Sleep my love, sleep. Sleep. [*whispering*] Sleep. [*hypnotizing*] Sleep, my dear. Sleep!

Kans: [*suddenly rising*] How can one sleep! How can one relax when everyone is predicting his death and praying for that prediction to come true? [*He counts on the fingers of both of his hands.*] One, two, three, four, five, six, seven, eight... [*He forms a lotus flower with the fingers of his hands.*] One, two, three, four, five, six, seven, eight... now this is the eighth. Which is the eighth? Any of these is the eighth? Eighth...or one of the eight, any one.
[*Pralamb, Baahuk and Pradyot kneel down before Kans.*]

All Three: [*in sinister, secretive whispers*] The Yaadav have been defeated. Whoever dared to raise his head was beheaded. Whoever dared to gaze had his eyes plucked out.

Kans: [*fearfully*] Any one of the eight, any one of them.

All Three: The Yaadav have been defeated, but their hopes are alive. Their will has not been broken.

Kans: Any one out of the eight, any one...

All Three: [*murmuring*] Kill Devakee. The root of the trouble will be removed. That way, the Yaadav's hopes will be shattered.

Kans: [*screaming*] No. This is not possible. How can I kill Devakee? I don't have the strength, nor even the desire to do so. I do not want this Kingdom, sovereignty or power.

[*Ugrasen's taunt 'This son of mine is a woman in the guise of a man'—is heard from backstage.*]

Yes. Kill Devakee.

[*He strikes the gong with a hammer. Pralamb, Pradyot and Baahuk turn their backs to the audience and stand in a row in the background.*]

Bring Devakee here.

[*The Guard leaves. Pralamb, Pradyot and Baahuk bow and exit. Kans picks up a sword. Devakee comes in as a prisoner with a soldier accompanying her. Kans gazes at her fondly.*]

Devakee: The *Mahaaraaj* sent for me?

Kans: [*recovering from distraction*] Oh, yes. I sent for you. [*He throws down the sword.*]

Devakee: Why?

Kans: You wanted to see me, right? I received your message.

Devakee: Yes.

Kans: So speak.

Devakee: May I speak to *Mahaaraaj* Kans alone?
[*Kans does not reply.*]
[*tauntingly*]
Is the *Mahaaraaj* afraid of me? Of an unarmed, frail woman?
[*Kans signals to the soldier to go away, who then exits.*]

Kans: What do you want to tell me?

Devakee: I merely wanted to see…

Kans: To see?

Devakee: How my dear brother looks as a King of Kings.

Kans: So, have you seen?

Devakee: Yes, I have.

Kans: What did you see?

Devakee: I could not recognize my own brother.

Kans: Did you recognize him earlier?

Devakee: Perhaps not. I used to imagine that I did,

but today I realized that I did not.

Kans: It's your own fault.

Devakee: Yes. It is. I should have known that the affection of a brother who jumped into a river to retrieve the doll of his darling sister would be false. But how was it that you risked your life like that?

[*Kans is silent.*]

Say something. Answer.

Kans: That was not false.

Devakee: Then is jailing your newly married sister and her husband just a show?

Kans: No.

Devakee: What is it then?

Kans: Both are true. Risking my life for my darling sister's sake, as well as subjecting her to the torture of prison.

Devakee: What are you?

Kans: You can see for yourself.

Devakee: An enigma?

Kans: No…a man.

Devakee: Is a man like this?

Kans: Yes, he is.

Devakee: Demon-like?

Kans: Yes, demon-like and god-like, too. This is the dilemma of a human being—split into a god and a devil—half and half. [*moving closer*] As soon as I saw my flower-like sister, I was moved to shower her with affection.

Devakee: [*choked with emotion*] Brother…[*She weeps with her head on Kans' chest.*]

Kans: [*patting her*] Cry, sister. Cry. [*wiping her tears*] This brother will not be able to give you anything except torture, prison and pain. Cry, my darling sister. [*He breaks into silent sobs and tears.*]

Devakee: [*wiping Kans' tears with the edge of her garment*] Don't cry, my brother…don't. I'm fine with it.

Kans: [*regaining composure*] Trying to console me? [*affectionately*] Silly girl!

Devakee: You chose my husband for me.

Kans: Yes, I chose Vasudev for you. You liked him very much, didn't you?

Devakee: [*bashfully*] He was your friend, that's why.

Kans: Devakee, I remember everything. Vasudev and I were such good friends. We used to race horses along the banks of the river Yamuna every evening. Once, while returning from the temple, you saw us and asked, 'Who was he? Who was with you?' I said, 'Vasudev.' Upon hearing his name, you blushed.

Devakee: What else do you remember?

Kans: Someone asked a seven-year-old girl, 'Whom do you like best?' Without thinking for even a second, she replied, 'Brother Kans.'

Devakee: Then, what is her crime?

Kans: She loves my enemy. She is the wife of my enemy.

Devakee: The enemy who was once a friend.

Kans: [*sternly*] Yes, 'once' a friend. It's an old tale but today it is meaningless.

Devakee: Brother! You are mistaken. He is not your enemy.

Kans: Do you know something I don't?

Devakee: Our tiny Yaadav Kingdom is situated between the two giant empires of Hastinaapur and Magadh. Magadh's King Jaraasandh wanted to conquer Mathuraa and merge it into his empire. But the King of Hastinaapur's promise of help prevented

King Jaraasandh's ambition from being fulfilled. Vasudev's efforts secured the King of Hastinaapur's assurance. That is why the King of Magadh is angry with him.

Kans: [*tauntingly*] Your husband told you all this?

Devakee: Yes.

Kans: Then has he not told you that his sister Kunti's husband, the King of Hastinaapur himself, wants to stake a claim over the small territory of Mathuraa?

Devakee: That is a lie.

Kans: If you had to choose between brother and husband, I know whose side you would take.

Devakee: I am telling you the truth!

Kans: [*sternly*] Your truth is whatever your husband tells you. He wanted to deprive me of my right over Mathuraa with Hastinaapur's help, and dreamt of becoming its ruler. He was hatching this conspiracy, which I completely crushed.

Devakee: With the help of the Magadh soldiers.

Kans: [*irritated*] Yes, with the help of the Magadh soldiers. Are the Hastinaapur soldiers any better than the Magadh soldiers? They are both exactly the same. No matter how small the Yaadav Kingdom may be, sandwiched between two giant entities, it has its own identity. I'll protect it till the last drop of my blood.

Devakee: He does not want the Kingdom of Mathuraa.

Kans: How can I believe that?

Devakee: Trust me.

Kans: Trust you?

Devakee: Yes, trust me. Believe me, I'm your sister... Trust me. [*sentimental*] Your darling sister's doll fell into the river—won't you risk your life once more and...?

Kans: Devakee, don't forget you are a prisoner. You are talking to the ruler of the Yaadav. Trust? What is the meaning of this word? You came to see me; our meeting is over now. [*He sounds the gong.*] You saw a god, now see the demon too. So you will never be mistaken.
[*The Guard enters.*]

Kans: Return the captive to prison.
[*Devakee bows and is about to exit.*]

Kans: Wait.
[*Devakee stops.*]

Kans: Listen carefully. The base of power is never

founded on trust. [*Pause.*] Now, you may go. [*Devakee and the Guard exit. Kans stands rooted in his place. Asti enters with a glass of wine in her hand. She pulls Kans by the arm towards herself.*]

Asti: Come, let's go to bed. I'm sleepy.

Kans: Then you please go to bed.

Asti: [*seductively*] Without you? How will I sleep? [*She tries to drag him with her again.*] Come, let's go.

Kans: [*explodes angriliy*] Please go away!

Asti: [*tauntingly*] The ruler of Mathuraa can be so scared.

Kans: I'm scared?

Asti: Indeed.

Kans: [*assertively*] I am not scared.

Asti: Really?

Kans: [*angrily*] I am not afraid.

Asti: Forgive me, *Mahaaraaj*. You are not afraid.

Kans: You think I'm afraid?

Asti: No.

Kans: You don't believe me?

Asti: I do.

Kans: [*strongly*] I am not afraid.

Asti: Yes, indeed…you aren't afraid.

Kans: Are you mocking me?

Asti: No.

Kans: You think I am a fool!

Asti: What?

Kans: The way you're smiling.

Asti: [*bored*] Oh!

Kans: You dare laugh at me!

Asti: I didn't laugh.

Kans: You're lying.

Asti: I did not laugh at you.

Kans: Such audacity! [*raging*] I…I will….

Asti: [*sharply*] What will you do?

Kans: You are vain because of your father, but I shall….

Asti: [*angrily*] Yes, I am vain because of my father. I was laughing at you. I will laugh even more. What can you do? If I had known you could be so scared, I would have brought more of my father's soldiers from Magadh. [*She haughtily exits while looking at Kans scornfully. Kans looks defeated as he sees her leave.*]

Kans: [*regaining composure*] Pradyot! Baahuk! Pralamb!
[*All three enter and stand before him, bowing.*]

Kans: Pradyot! All the prominent leaders of the Andhak, Vrishni, Bhoj and Shoor tribes of the Yaadav have to be kept under surveillance. They are all enemies. They all pose great danger for us. Do not trust anyone. Security measures must be strengthened.

Pradyot: Your orders shall be executed.

Kans: Baahuk will assist you. [*to Pralamb*] Pralamb, I want you to gather information about every household—about what goes on in there—from the husband about the wife, from the wife about the husband.

Pralamb: Lord, your orders shall be obeyed.

Kans: You may go now.
[*All three bow and are about to leave.*]

Kans: [*impatiently*] Pradyot!
[*Baahuk and Pralamb exit; only Pradyot remains.*]
[*after a few moments*] In whom can I place my trust?

Pradyot: Is there no one in whom you can....

Kans: There is only one.

Pradyot: Who?

Kans: Pradyot.

Pradyot: [*excitedly*] Kans! I will do anything for you. Maybe we were related to each other in our previous births.

Kans: Maybe...

Pradyot: When you meet certain people, you feel as if they are your own. You are prepared to do anything, even lay down your life for them.
[*Kans smiles indulgently at Pradyot.*]

Pradyot: Your smile is so becoming. It can enslave anyone. I have admired it for ages, since you were twelve.

Kans: Pradyot, the Yaadav army is under you. My life is in your hands.

Pradyot: As long as I am alive, no harm will come to you.

Kans: You may go now, Pradyot.

Pradyot: [*while leaving*] Please rest assured... [*He turns to go.*]

Kans: Pradyot!
[*Pradyot stops.*]

Kans: Does the army chief not bow before leaving the presence of the King?

Pradyot: Pardon, my Lord. [*He bows.*]

Kans: I can't trust Pralamb. Keep an eye on him.

Pradyot: Your wish shall be obeyed. [*He bows again and exits.*]
[*The Guard enters.*]

Guard: Devee Swaati is here.

Kans: Send her in.
[*The Guard bows and exits. Swaati enters.*]

Swaati: Why have you sent for me?

Kans: Have you seen this royal palace?

Swaati: You sent for me to give me a tour of the palace?

Kans: Yes.

Swaati: You want to impress me?

Kans: No. I want to show you how your lover

Kans is imprisoned here.

Swaati: The Princess of Magadh must have created a heaven here.

Kans: But I need you, Swaati.

Swaati: Every king wants to expand his harem.

Kans: [*as if hurt*] Swaati! [*after pausing*] Try to understand me. I am all alone at the pinnacle of power. There is no one I can rely upon. Swaati, I beg your help.

Swaati: How can I help you?

Kans: I will tell you.

Swaati: No Kans. I can't do anything.

Kans: [*coming closer and looking into her eyes*] Everyone wants to kill your Kans. You want to see his head chopped off?

Swaati: Don't say such a terrible thing.

Kans: If you have truly loved me, then promise that you will do what I tell you.

Swaati: I will, in any case, do what you want. Where's the need to promise?

Kans: [*insistently*] Still, Swaati….

Swaati: Alright, I promise. I'll do anything for you.

Kans: I want you to...you to....

Swaati: If I had known that the path of love was so full of thorns, I would have never stepped upon it. [*tauntingly*] Ask me whatever you wish. I am bound by oath and I am madly in love with you. You'll never get such an opportunity again. Ask me.

Kans: I want...I want...

Swaati: Speak up.

Kans: I want you to marry Pradyot.

Swaati: [*Swaati is frozen in stunned silence*] [*after a while*] Since I have given you my word, I can even marry a stone at your bidding.

Kans: I can't trust Pradyot despite my best attempts. I want you to observe him all the time and keep me informed. [*pleading*] It's a matter of life or death for me.

Swaati: I shall do as you say. Worshippers of the god of love are as blind as he is. [*The Guard enters.*]

Guard: [*bowing*] Army Chief Pradyot is here.

Kans: Let him enter. [*Pradyot enters with a bow.*]

Kans: Pradyot, this is Swaati, our most trusted

Yaadav girl. I want you to accept her as your wife.
[*Pradyot eyes Swaati for a moment.*]

Pradyot: Your wish is most welcome, my Lord.
[*Kans draws Swaati's veil down over her face. Then he takes hold of Pradyot's arm, brings him to Swaati and places her hand in his.*]

Kans: You may take your bride. Your marriage will be celebrated all over the Kingdom.

[*Pradyot and Swaati bow to Kans and make their exit with Pradyot escorting her out.*]

Flashback v ends

Kans: Can I ever forget Swaati, even though I gave her away to Pradyot? Shall I ever forget her? Even after so many years' absence, she comes suddenly, like a whiff of spring in autumn, quietly, stealthily, with light steps, and pushes open the doors of past memories—that lively teenager, bouncing doe, enchanting like *Rati*, the Goddess of love.

FLASHBACK VI BEGINS

[*The forest part of the stage is illuminated. Swaati comes running up to Kans, panting.*]

Swaati: He ran away. See, he fled!

Kans: Who?

Swaati: The young deer. So naughty—one just can't catch him. He harasses me like crazy. See, he's hidden there in the grove. I am fed up with looking for him. [*suddenly*] Look, there he is. He is peeping at me with his head thrust out of the bushes. He takes pleasure in teasing me. Just look.

Kans: [*looking at Swaati*] I am looking.

Swaati: Not at me! Look at the young deer.

Kans: I am looking at the doe.

Swaati: [*ignoring him*] Oh! How beautiful!

Kans: Indeed, how beautiful!

Swaati: Just look at his eyes; how brilliantly black they are.

Kans: Black like beetles sitting on the white petals of a lotus; like fish wriggling in a blue pond.

Swaati: [*staring back at Kans*] Don't look at me like that.

Kans: I want to dive into your eyes, into the depths of your heart where there isn't anyone but me.

Swaati: You are already there.

Kans: Only me and no one else.

Swaati: But don't look at me like that. [*Imploring*] Not like that.

Kans: [*holding her by both her arms*] Swaati!

Swaati: Don't look at me like that.

Kans: Swaati!

Swaati: Don't. I see your eyes asking for something; I am too weak. I won't be able to refuse you. No, I am going away. [*Moves slightly away from Kans, but stops suddenly.*] Let me go, Kans.

Kans: I have not stopped you.

Swaati: You did stop me.

Kans: I have not said a word.

Swaati: Does everything need to be said with words? [*Kans does not respond.*]

Swaati: Without speaking, one can say a lot. I am very weak. Let me go. [*Kans moves closer to Swaati.*]

Kans: Swaati!

Swaati: Kans! [*She runs into Kans' open arms and gets*

locked into an embrace.]

[*The stage becomes dark. After a moment, one ray of dawn rises in the sky, along with the sound of birds chirping. Kans is sleeping on the ground under a tree. Swaati is seen coming back from bathing in a nearby lake, with a few flowers in her hands. Her hair is loose and spread across her back.*]

Swaati: [*gently brushing Kans' face with a flower*] Get up now.

Kans: [*opening his eyes*] Swaati!

Swaati: [*kissing the flower*] Look at how lovely the vermilion of the morning sky is.
[*Kans pulls her to himself in an embrace.*]

Swaati: [*freeing herself*] Now release me, Arch-Prince. I'm already late.
[*Kans sits up and buries his face in Swaati's hair, inhaling with relish.*]

Kans: I've made a discovery.

Swaati: What's that?

Kans: Heaven is right here.

Swaati: If my father finds out about this, you will discover that hell is right here!

Kans: Swaati, you need not fear. You are mine and I promise…

Swaati: [*covering his mouth with her hand*] No Kans, don't. I don't want promises.

Kans: But I…

Swaati: Between you and me, there is only love. Love and trust. Don't tarnish it with a promise.

Kans: [*tenderly*] Swaati!

Swaati: Now, let's forget all this. I'm getting late. Please fasten the backstrings of my top.

Kans: Oh…I don't know how to do it.

Swaati: You know how to undo it! Who else will do it? Tie it.

Kans: [*playfully, with exaggerated humility*] Your command shall be carried out.
[*He ties it.*]

Swaati: A little while ago when I woke up, I found you sleeping with your head nestled on my arm. I felt that, despite your large body, you were just a child—innocent and unprotected…Is the womb of a woman the core of her being? Of her physical, mental and emotional consciousness? I wanted to nestle your head against my breasts. Then I feared you might wake up, so I stopped myself. When I somehow pulled my arm out from under your head and strolled towards the lake, I felt...as if my head was touching the sky. Everything was the same, as always. The centuries-old familiar sky; the same earth, the same dew-drenched grass that wets the feet, the spreading red color of dawn on the treetops. Only I had changed. I was not who I used to be. You have transformed me by touching me somewhere in the core of my being. I encountered a new horizon of life with your love. A shimmering rainbow of some enchanting world seemed to be embracing every ripple of my body. I lacked the courage to examine my own reflection in the water. My appearance may have changed, which could reveal what I had secretly found. I stood there, thinking for god only knows how long. At last, I gathered enough courage to look at my own reflection. To my utter surprise, the same familiar face stared back at me. Nothing had changed. I was just as I was. I was filled with an unexpected dismay—with anger. Why hadn't my appearance changed? Why was I still the same? Why should the boundless, inexpressible, unspeakable joy and thrill of which I had become the mistress be limited to me? I wanted the whole world to know about this happiness. Why didn't some telltale signs appear upon my face saying, 'This is Swaati, who now belongs to Kans?'

Kans: As what?

Swaati: [*looking into his eyes*] As his beloved. [*Blushing, she gets up and moves away from*

Kans, and then turns to him.] You must think I'm so immodest. [*clinging to Kans*] But you give me dignity. I do not feel shy with you. [*hesitatingly*]...But I can't understand...

Kans: What?

Swaati: The invisible bond between two people... two bodies—the yearning to possess that transcends possession of one another, the tangled pain of satiety and desire, the tide of attraction drowning the separateness of physical entities and the passionate music of mingled breaths...[*She disappears behind a tree.*]

Flashback vi ends

Kans: [*coming forward on the stage*] I, too, do not understand it, Swaati. I still haven't understood it, even after so many years have passed—this invisible bond of attraction and attachment.

FLASHBACK VII BEGINS

[*'Don't delay further, O, Deliverer!' The chorus is heard singing this from the wings.*]

Kans: Who is this deliverer? [*vaingloriously*] I, *Mahaaraaj* Kans, can raise a pebble of earth and make it a star in the sky. I can pluck stars from the sky and grind them to dust. My enemies tremble like dry leaves in a storm. The trumpet call of my army shakes the throne of God Indr. The all-

powerful *Mahaaraaj* Kans, King of Kings... [*as if his ability to speak disappears, haltingly*] Deliverer? Who is this deliverer?
[*Pralamb enters.*]

Pralamb: The deliverer is fictitious.

Kans: I'll destroy this fiction.

Pralamb: You cannot destroy it.

Kans: Why not?

Pralamb: As long as a single person lives, this fiction will continue to live on in his mind.

Kans: In that case, not a single person shall remain alive.

Pralamb: Who will the King of Kings rule then?
[*Kans doesn't reply.*]

Pralamb: The religious beliefs, discourses and teachings of holy men have been engraved upon the minds of the people, like writing on a granite stone, that in their time of difficulties, God will take human form and appear on earth to free them from misery.

Kans: [*concluding*] So these are my real enemies?

Pralamb: Yes, holy men, religious teachings....

Kans: But...

Pralamb: Seven of Devakee's sons have already been sent to heaven by your Highness...

Kans: So what?

Pralamb: All seven times, the Yaadav women felt as if part of their wombs had been snatched out and trampled upon. The Yaadav have suppressed the rage in their hearts seven times, and offerings have been made in temples seven times for the incarnation of God.

Kans: For my destruction? [*scornfully*] Fools!

Pralamb: King of Kings, a theatre group from Kashi is very popular these days amongst the people of Mathuraa.

Kans: Theater group?

Pralamb: It's been in Mathuraa for the past six months, and the people are not tiring of seeing it.

Kans: Have you seen it? What's it about?

Pralamb: After seeing it, the *Mahaaraaj* will be able to assess its popularity for himself.

Kans: Then I will watch it.

Pralamb: As you please, my Lord! [*He bows and leaves.*]

[*Kans goes to sit on the throne. Pradyot and Pralamb come from outside and stand near him. The Guard stands with his head bowed. Pralamb motions to the Guard, who then goes to summon the theatre group.*]

Pralamb: King of Kings, the play that will be presented by this theatre group is called "*Narasingh* Avataar," that is "the incarnation of *Narasingh*." He who is half man, half lion.

Kans: You said that this is highly popular amongst the people?

Pralamb: It is so popular that though it has been staged for the last six months, people continue to make a mad rush to see it. That is why the troupe is not leaving Mathuraa anytime soon.

Kans: If what you say about them is true, [*cryptically*] they will never leave Mathuraa.

Guard: Glory be to His Highness, the King of Kings. The theatre group has arrived.

[*The Narrator and his two Assistants, one man and one woman, enter. Both Assistants are wearing masks. One of the Assistants holds a sheet in his hand. All three prostrate themselves before Kans. Kans extends his right hand over them, as if to bless them.*]

Pralamb: [*to the Assistants*] The King of Kings has made your lives full with his blessings. [*to*

Narrator] Now, present the opera....
[*The Narrator rises and folds his hands. Both of his Assistants stand behind him holding the sheet spread out like a curtain.*]

Chorus: O, God Shiva Shanker! The innocent one!
Have mercy on us;
O Deliverer of this world!
Carry my boat to the shore.

Narrator: Long, long ago...
There was a city that turned against God.
Its King was Hiranyakashipu.
[*The Assistants place the curtain on the floor, revealing Hiranyakashipu wearing a ferocious mask of a lion. He mimes, following the Narrator's recitation.*]

Narrator: Under Hiranyakashipu's tyrannical rule, the people's misery became unbearable.
That irreligious and vile king
From the pride of power
From the glitter of gold
He forgot himself.
Forgot religion and God;
Started acting arbitrarily.
He forgot that
A king looks after his subjects
As a father looks unto his sons.
He plundered the people
Filled his coffers
Crushed the subjects
And raised high, higher and still higher
His throne upon their corpses.

Whoever dared lift his eyes was turned blind
Whoever dared raise his arms was soon without them
Whoever dared raise his voice was throttled
Whoever dared move forward was pushed back

Whoever wished to run away, could not do so
Whoever wanted to live, could not do so
Whoever wanted to die, could not do so
Dying while still alive

Dying every moment of one's life
Helplessness, suffocation...
Over all this ruled and reigned
Like a sky-kissing tower
On the foundation of corpses
Hiranyakashipu.

Chorus: O, God! Compassionate one!
Giver of grace, full of benediction.
All-powerful, the greatest.
Strength of the weak.
Home of the homeless.

Narrator: Hear our screams, wailings and lamentations. Protect us. We are at your mercy. O friend of the poor, save us from Hiranyakashipu's tyranny. Be merciful. Hiranyakashipu is selfish. For his own ends, he can perform the worst misdeeds. Disagreeing with him is misconstrued as rebellion. He has usurped his subjects' wealth to fill his treasury.

He has deprived the peasants of their land, the women of their ornaments and the traders of their money—even the dead of their shrouds. Only the sycophants, the selfish and godless, are flourishing in his Kingdom. Under the guise of Hiranyakashipu's name, they have become even more tyrannical.

O compassionate one…where are you? You've taken too long to come. We can't bear this any longer. The pain, the misery, this life that's even worse than death, have become insufferable. Life has no meaning when one is dying every moment, part by part, bit by bit.

Assistants: [*crying*] Save us! Save us! Save us!

Narrator: Just then, a prophecy was heard from the sky…
[*The Assistants lower the curtain, revealing Lord Vishnu.*]

Lord Vishnu: Devoted ones, have patience. The pot of sins is full to the brim. I shall soon take birth on this earth and bring deliverance.
[*The curtain is raised and Lord Vishnu disappears.*]

Narrator: Upon hearing this prophecy, hope blossomed again in the withered hearts of the people. A tide of joy swept the villages.
[*Both Assistants dance in joyful abandon.*]

Narrator: [*as the dance ends*] After this prophecy, the subjects of that godless Kingdom waited day and night for the avataar's arrival.

Assistants: Hiranyakashipu became even more tyrannical to crush peoples' hope for the avataar. But belief in the avataar grew stronger, despite the increasing tyranny. [*in a joyful tone*] And witness this wonder! Just as a lotus grows in mud, an ascetic is born in a demon's house! [*Prahlaad is seen praying with folded hands as the Assistants lower the curtain.*]

Assistants: He was named Prahlaad. The first word that he uttered was the name of God. The King of that godless State was perplexed. The King's sycophants were baffled. What was this miracle? No one could understand. [*The Assistants raise the curtain in front of Prahlaad.*]

Narrator: At last, Hiranyakashipu's anger was roused.
As if a sleeping lion had awakened.
As if a dormant volcano had erupted.
He tried to make Prahlaad see reason.
He threatened.
Had him thrown down a hill.
Had him burnt in fire.
But...
Not a hair of his head was harmed.

Chorus: O Shiva Shanker! Glory be to you. Oh, kind one! Take pity on us. Deliverer of this world, carry my boat to the shore.

Narrator: In the end, the demon came to kill the innocent child who was tied to an iron pillar, with a bare sword. [*The Assistants lower the screen. Prahlaad can be seen, bound to an iron pillar with a chain. Hiranyakashipu is standing close to him with a naked sword.*]

Hiranyakashipu: I can take your life at any minute.

Prahlaad: Life and death are in the hands of God.

Hiranyakashipu: Fool, I am the dispenser of your life and death. I am God.

Prahlaad: Your conceit is ill-founded.

Hiranyakashipu: Alright, call your God then. Let me see how he protects you. You'll witness your death at my hands.
[*Hiranyakashipu raises his hand to kill. Just then, there is a loud, explosive sound. Narasingh bursts out from the pillar. He catches and holds Hiranyakashipu by his stomach. Blood flows from Hiranyakashipu's stomach.*]

Kans: [*screaming*] Stop it! [*He sounds the gong three times. It resounds menacingly.*]
[*Three Hangmen wearing black robes with their faces covered by black facemasks revealing only their eyes, emerge from three corners.*]

Kans: From today onward, plays are banned in the Yaadav Kingdom.
[*There is an echo in the atmosphere.*]

Kans: From today onward, Gods will not be

worshipped in this Kingdom.
[*Another echo is heard.*]

Kans: These actors appear to be agents of Hastinaapur. For the sake of the security of the Yaadav Kingdom and its people, these Yaadav enemies will be publicly hanged.
[*The actors are frozen speechless with fear. The three Hangmen take them away at the point of their spears. Baahuk runs in.*]

Baahuk: The Yaadav have revolted. When our Magadh soldiers pushed them, they hid themselves in temples. The soldiers have set the temples on fire. Look at the flames!
[*Leaping flames are projected on the cyclorama.*]

Kans: I am pleased with you, Baahuk. [*He takes off one of his necklaces and gives it to Baahuk.*] Power flows from the sharp edge of a sword.
[*The flames suddenly become brighter. The cries and shrieks of panicky people fill the atmosphere.*]

Flashback vii ends

CURTAIN

'THE KING OF MATHURAA ': Photographs from an earlier production in India

'THE KING OF MATHURAA ': Photographs from an earlier production in India

Act Two

FLASHBACK VIII BEGINS

[*When the curtain rises, the stage is seen as before. Kans is sitting on the throne. Pralamb is standing nearby.*]

Pralamb: As per your command, music is now prohibited in Mathuraa. The temples have become deserted. Dogs and swines gallivant there. The Yaadav Kingdom has banished God, yet…

Kans: Yet…?

Pralamb: God has been driven out of the temples, but not yet from the Yaadav Kingdom.

Kans: Where is he now?

Pralamb: In the hearts and homes of the Yaadav.

Kans: I will pluck out their hearts and set fire to their homes.

Pralamb: The foolish masses cannot live without God.

Kans: They will have to manage.

Pralamb: God sustains the masses. He instills fear in their hearts, but also gives hope for a golden future. People live by God.

Kans: [*contemplating*] I will give them a new God.

Pralamb: A new God?

Kans: King Kans can become God *Shree* Kans and be enshrined in the temples.

Pralamb: God *Shree* Kans!

Kans: People can place Kans on the throne of their hearts as God, in both of his forms, that of the benign protector and the angry destroyer.

Pralamb: [*understanding*] I am at the feet of God *Shree* Kans.

Kans: [*musing*] God *Shree* Kans. [*determined*] Let it be declared that from today onward, in the Kingdom of Mathuraa, God *Shree* Kans alone will be worshipped. Only God *Shree* Kans. He who defies this shall be put to death. The devoted shall know the grace of God *Shree* Kans and will be bestowed with prosperity in this world as well as in the next.

Pralamb: Your orders shall be executed. [*He bows and exits.*]

Kans: God *Shree* Kans! [*laughing loudly*] God! Effeminate Kans! King of Kings Kans! God *Shree* Kans! [*He laughs aloud again.*] God! [*Pradyot enters.*]

Pradyot: My Lord, the sacred idols of God *Shree* Kans have been installed in temples and all the prominent places of the city, crossings, squares and gardens. The masses are collecting by the thousands in temples to have a 'holy glimpse.' Priests are being appointed in various temples to worship God *Shree* Kans. Groups of divine hymn singers have been sent to different parts of the state. Five hundred and one priests are reciting the name of God *Shree* Kans in the City Square.

Kans: I am pleased with this arrangement, Pradyot. [*Pradyot bows and exits. Pralamb enters with a lamp in hand.*]

Pralamb: This is for your *aarati.* From this one lamp, hundreds and thousands more lamps shall be lit. The citizens of Mathuraa will feel blessed and be freed of their sins from many lives. [*He performs an aarati of Kans.*]

Kans: Pralamb, from today onward, I appoint you High Priest of the Kans religion.
[*Pralamb bows and exits.*]
[*to himself*] Coward! Effeminate! King of Kings! God *Shree* Kans…and now Kans religion!
[*Baahuk enters with a poor, frightened fisherman and bows.*]

Baahuk: This fisherman will tell you about the greatness of the name of God *Shree* Kans.

Fisherman: [*repeating what he has memorized*] Lord, I was fishing in the river. Suddenly the current became too swift. The sand under my feet gave way, and I was swept away. I started screaming. I was about to die. Just then, I started reciting your divine name. And a miracle happened! My feet touched the ground. I was saved from drowning. I came out of death's clutches by the grace of God *Shree* Kans' name.
[*Kans removes a ring off his finger and gives it to him.*]

Kans: Give him one hundred silver coins from the Royal Treasury.
[*Baahuk bows. The fisherman prostrates. Both exit.*]

Flashback viii ends

FLASHBACK IX BEGINS

[*Sounds of a storm in the background. Swaati enters, carrying a newborn baby in her arms. Pralamb, Pradyot and Baahuk accompany her.*]

Kans: [*with demonic joy*] My destroyer! Devakee's eighth son!

Swaati: It is a girl.

Kans: Girl? [*He stands lost in thought for a minute, then forms a lotus with the fingers of both his hands.*] Eighth child or any one of the eight. [*He suddenly snatches the baby from Swaati's hands and raises her high, in preparation to dash her to the ground.*]

Swaati: [*nervously*] It's a girl. Even she…?

Kans: Swaati, everything is fair in love and war. [*He dashes the child to the ground. A loud explosive sound and a blaze of lightning cross the sky.*]

Kans: Did you hear? Did you people hear? Did you see? She rose to the sky as a Goddess and said, 'Your destroyer was sent elsewhere after birth.'

Pradyot: No, my God!

Kans: You did not see anything?

Pradyot: No.

Kans: Pralamb, did you?
[*Pralamb shakes his head*]

Kans: Baahuk, did you not see anything either?

Baahuk: No, my God!

Kans: That dazzling ball of light in the dark midnight sky...That goddess-like form?

Baahuk: God, I did not see anything at all.

Kans: And you, Swaati? Did you hear that prophecy?

Swaati: Yes, I did.

Kans: [*pleased*] You did?

Swaati: Not the prophecy.

Kans: Then?

Swaati: The voice of fear from the heart of God *Shree* Kans.

Kans: [*hurt*] Swaati! [*shouting*] Get out of here. All of you...
[*All bow and exit.*]

Flashback ix ends

[*The storm becomes more violent.*]

Kans: The storm raging in my heart more than matches the fierce storm outside. Mistrust, doubts, fear from all sides assail me. Swaati was correct. My fear-ridden heart has created the prophecy. The fear that pervades every atom of my being created that goddess, which only I… and no one else…could see.
[*The storm stops.*]

Kans: I knew for sure that Devakee's eighth son was never born. But I also knew the peoples' belief. They had such faith in that prophecy that whoever does kill me will be regarded by the people as Devakee's eighth son. I therefore ordered that Swaati may see to it that all children born on the eighth day of the dark half of the month of *'Saawan'* be killed. I had hoped that this may break the peoples' belief in the incarnation of a God to destroy me. But the peoples' blind faith was not shaken.

FLASHBACK X BEGINS

[*Pralamb enters.*]

Pralamb: My God, the Yaadav people think that Krishna, the son of Nand and chief of Gokul village, is the incarnation of God.

Kans: Chief Nand. Has he paid his dues?

Pralamb: He deposits his dues to the Royal Treasury much before the deadline. He is foremost in demonstrating faith in God. He has even established a temple dedicated to God *Shree* Kans in Gokul village. It's difficult to bring any kind of charge against him. And if you do take any action against him, the Yaadav are bound to become unhappy.

Kans: Then Swaati will do this work.

[*Pralamb bows and exits. The Guard enters.*]

Guard: Glory be to the royal God. Devee Swaati seeks an audience.

[*Kans assents and the Guard exits. Swaati enters.*]

Kans: Swaati! [*He tries to hold her in his arms.*]

Swaati: [*freeing herself*] In your embrace I start forgetting….

Kans: What?

Swaati: Nothing.

Kans: What do you start forgetting?

Swaati: That you are the glorious, the bravest and most powerful King of Kings, the highest, the mightiest God *Shree* Kans.

Kans: Are you mocking me?

Swaati: And I, for a moment, recall Kans the lover, in the first flush of his youth.

Kans: I still love you.

Swaati: Sounds nice, even though it's a lie.

Kans: You mock…

Swaati: [*cutting his sentence short*] No.

Kans: I'm so lonely, caught up in this whirl of power…so very alone! No friends…no one to help me, no one in whom I can trust. Despite this loneliness there is, in one corner of my heart, the knowledge that I am not alone. At least Swaati is there...

Swaati: My Lord, what is your command?

Kans: Lord! Command?

Swaati: Should I address you as something else? [*In an attempt to placate Swaati, Kans tries to embrace her.*]

Kans: Swaati, you are…

Swaati: [*freeing herself*] You had a dream during the first flush of your youth. To make this dream come true, the first person you sacrificed was Swaati. She is now dead.

Kans: In that sacrificial fire, Kans was also reduced to ashes.

Swaati: Yes, a lover was burnt to death, but...

Kans: But?

Swaati: From that sacred fire of the *Yagn*, arose the King of Kings, God *Shree* Kans. [*tauntingly*] The brightest, the bravest, the most powerful, King of Kings, the Highest God *Shree* Kans!

Kans: [*impatiently*] Oh, Swaati! [*with self-pity*] You are so heartless. Can't you feel any pity for me?

Swaati: [*emotionless*] Give me a command.

Kans: There is a village close to Mathuraa, [*pausing*] called Gokul.

Swaati: I know that place.

Kans: Yaadav believe that Krishna, one of the sons of its chief, Nand, is the incarnation of Lord Vishnu. They have been hoping for years that some incarnation would appear for the purpose of Kans' destruction. In order to liberate themselves from the tyrannical and oppressive rule of the heartless Kans, people are ready to regard illusory hope as truth.

Swaati: At your bidding, I have had so many children of the Mathuraa Kingdom killed.

Kans: But their hope has not been shattered.

Swaati: Will it break by this one more murder?

Kans: No. As long as Kans is here, with his despotic rule and tyranny, the blind hope of getting rid of him will remain. Even after the murder of these children, this hope has not died out. After Krishna's death, people will come to regard yet another as Lord Vishnu's incarnation.

Swaati: Then why this murder?

Kans: Does one stop living because one day he shall die?

Swaati: I did not mean that.

Kans: This is a game. We are all bound by the rules of the game. These rules are, probably, the game itself

[*Swaati looks as if she does not understand him.*]

Kans: —that Kans should tyrannize and that the subjects should dream of liberation. Both are bound by the rules of the game. As long as we exist, we cannot help but play along.

Swaati: Until when?

Kans: Until only one of us is left. Kans can't help but destroy all the Krishnas that are born. The game demands it.

Swaati: Why not withdraw from the game?

Kans: Do you wish that your Kans flees from the battlefield?

Swaati: [*giving up*] You just don't understand.

Kans: Until only one of us is left.

Swaati: A few days ago, my son [*voice breaking emotionally*]...my only son, died.

Kans: [*sympathetically*] I know?

Swaati: Do you know how I feel?

Kans: How?

Swaati: My women spies, out of deference to your wishes, killed so many children in Mathuraa Kingdom. It's so horrifying that people have started saying that I am a sorceress who has giant teeth and nails and sucks the blood of children. They have also given me a new name: Pootnaa! Pootnaa!! [*dispassionately*] I did all this for your sake. To see you happy.

Kans: I know, Swaati.

Swaati: To frighten their children, their mothers tell them that Pootnaa is coming. To make her lover's dream come true, sweetheart Swaati has become the sorceress Pootnaa.

Kans: Swaati!

Swaati: Swaati is a sorceress! She is Pootnaa, the killer of children! [*She starts laughing, which gradually turns into sobbing.*]

Kans: [*sympathetically*] Swaati! [*He lays a hand on one of her shoulders.*]

Swaati: [*suddenly*] No, Kans, I cannot do it.

Kans: [*entreating*] Swaati!

Swaati: I am a mother too. The mother in me cannot be completely suppressed. Besides, I am very tired. I have followed you in this race for power, out of my fear of losing you. Now I cannot run anymore. I am completely exhausted.

Kans: I know.

Swaati: I have only one remaining desire. That I may rest, away from this mad race. Eternal rest.

Kans: I know.

Swaati: [*vehemently*] What do you know? Only that Swaati is a frail woman!

Kans: No.

Swaati: Then...?

Kans: Your love for Kans is a thing of the past now.

Swaati: [*scathingly*] This is all you make of it! [*Kans does not answer.*]

Swaati: Answer me. This is what you actually think? [*She laughs bitterly.*] What else can you think, after all? [*tauntingly*] The brightest, the most powerful, the bravest…

Kans: [*stopping her*] Swaati!

Swaati: For the one whose dreams I have given my life, I have crushed each dream of mine. To keep his love alive, I have sacrificed all my happiness… [*in a sudden, determined tone*] His Lordship's command shall be carried out. Swaati herself shall go to destroy Krishna.

Kans: I have not told you to go in person; any of your woman spies can…

Swaati: [*firmly*] Swaati will go to destroy Krishna herself.
[*Swaati strides out, determinedly. Kans gazes at her as she leaves. Pralamb enters.*]

Kans: Pralamb, did you see Devee Swaati?

Pralamb: I did, but she did not notice me. She seemed lost in thought. [*after a pause*] There was something else...

Kans: What?

Pralamb: I have never seen such divine peace on her face. It was as if there was a brilliant halo all around her.

Kans: [*to himself*] A brilliant halo around the face of

a sorceress!! [*to Pralamb*] Swaati is going to destroy Krishna of Gokul, herself.

Pralamb: [*surprised*] Herself?

Kans: Yes, herself. I want her to receive complete protection, so that no harm befalls her. You will make all possible security arrangements without letting her know.

Pralamb: My God, your command will be executed. [*He leaves with a bow.*]

Flashback x ends

Kans: [*to himself*] Delicate sentiments in the heart of flintlike, cruel and despotic Kans! All human beings have their limitations. A man may surge high in the sky, yet he is bound to the earth. Pools of cool water may be found beneath the desert lands. Thorny bushes also bear flowers. I have severed all connections, yet there are certain bonds that do not snap, even if so desired.

FLASHBACK XI BEGINS

[*Pralamb enters.*]

Kans: [*angrily*] Lies, nonsense. I can't accept all this. How is it possible?

Pralamb: The rumor has spread throughout the Yaadav kingdom, like wildfire. All regard Krishna as the incarnation of Lord Vishnu.

Kans: Fools! All are fools. A small baby like Krishna—how can he kill Devee Swaati? There is some conspiracy behind it. I suspect that you are also one of the conspirators.

Pralamb: [*fearfully*] No! No, my Royal God!

Kans: [*moving near Pralamb*] I sent you to guard her life. I'll punish you personally for not carrying out my orders. [*He starts strangling Pralamb.*] You wicked, vile traitor...

Pralamb: Before dying, I want to disclose a secret to you.

Kans: [*releasing his throat*] Secret? [*contemptuously*] We know the secret. The newborn baby sucked the life out of Devee Swaati's poisoned breasts. That's what you wanted to tell us, right?

Pralamb: No...

Kans: Then?

Pralamb: Something else.

Kans: What?

Pralamb: Devee Swaati did not smear her breasts with poison.

Kans: Impossible.

Pralamb: But she had a small packet of lethal poison with her.

Kans: So...?

Pralamb: She took out a pinch of that poison with one hand. Then she removed Krishna's mouth from her breast, opened it with her other hand to put poison in it, but...

Kans: [*impatiently*] The stupid Yaadav fools attacked her suddenly? And you, who were in charge of her security, were helpless?

Pralamb: No, Lord, that's not true...

Kans: [*impatiently*] What is it then? Tell me quickly. Don't speak in riddles! Tell me the truth.

Pralamb: Before putting poison into Krishna's mouth, Devee Swaati stopped for a split second, her eyes sparkling with maternal love and affection. She suddenly hugged Krishna and put the poison into her own mouth.

Kans: [*shouting*] That's a lie!

Pralamb: Royal God, I am willing to be punished.

Kans: [*with pathos*] Swaati! Swaati! Swaati!! You have also betrayed me. Everyone has betrayed me! You have deserted your Kans, Swaati! [*He bursts into tears.*]

Pralamb: Royal God!

Kans: [*regaining control*] Let it be known that the Royal God is extremely angry with the

misdeeds of sorceress Pootnaa. Pootnaa's dead body will be hung in the city square tomorrow before sunrise. The citizens must know that every killer of Yaadav children will be severely punished. God, the protector of devotees, has no mercy for such a sinful sorceress.
[*Pralamb bows and is about to leave.*]

Kans: Wait, Pralamb.
[*Kans comes close to him.*]

Kans: Pralamb, after Swaati's death, it is not wise to trust Pradyot. You are the most loyal person I know.

Pralamb: God is kind to me, indeed. [*He bows and exits.*]

Flashback xi ends

Kans: [*narrating*] After that, I decided that repression should be made less ruthless. About that time, I was invited by my father-in-law, Emperor Jaraasandh, the ruler of Magadh, to defend the horse of the *Ashvamedha Yagn*. It was an honor I could not decline. I handed the charge of Mathuraa to Pralamb and Pradyot and went away to Magadh. I conducted many battles there for many years, and made many other Kings place their crowns at the feet of the Magadh King. When I returned to Mathuraa, my father-in-law's favorite army chief, Vritrighn, also came with me.

FLASHBACK XII BEGINS

[Vritrighn enters and bows.]

Vritrighn: Glory be to the Lord of Mathuraa.

Kans: Vritrighn, how do you like our city Mathuraa?

Vritrighn: This city is unique in all of the three worlds. Its palaces, buildings embraced by the ever-flowing blue Yamuna river…

Kans: Vritrighn, you speak so pleasantly. Compared to your city, which is like an array of jewels, you like ours? You truly flatter us.

Vritrighn: But, Lord, what I'm about to tell you now is not very sweet.

Kans: [*after a moment's hesitation*] Speak. You have our permission.

Vritrighn: Lord, you are surrounded by enemies. Every Yaadav wishes you were dead. There is resentment and anger towards you in every section of the Yaadav. A rebellion could break out anytime.

Kans: Really?

Vritrighn: My Magadh spies who brought this

information are very competent and reliable.

Kans: Pralamb and Pradyot never told me anything.

Vritrighn: They side with the rebels.

Kans: Impossible!

Vritrighn: In your absence, the sprouted seed of rebellion has become a full-grown tree. The greatest danger is from the younger crowd—the youth.

Kans: Youth?

Vritrighn: Young men and women secretly gather at night, in forests and ruins. They practice wielding arms and plan strategies to foment resentment and hatred toward you. [*Kans sounds the gong. The Guard enters.*]

Kans: Send Pradyot.
[*The Guard leaves.*]

Kans: Who is their leader?

Vritrighn: Lord, you prohibited music in the Kingdom of Mathuraa; now every rebel carries a flute with him, as a sign of protest.

Kans: Flute?

Vritrighn: Yes, a flute. A symbol of their rebellion against the ban on music.

Kans: Who is their leader?

Vritrighn: Krishna.

Kans: [*recollecting*] Krishna! The son of the Yaadav chief Nand of Gokul village?

Vritrighn: Yes, the son of Nand. But the Yaadav consider him to be the eighth son of Devakee.

Kans: [*assuredly*] That's a lie! Superstition! Devakee never gave birth to the eighth son.

Vritrighn: If everyone starts believing in this superstitious falsehood, then in due course of time, it will become the truth.

Kans: I understand, Vritrighn.

Vritrighn: In the Mathuraa Kingdom, the notes of a flute are more forceful than the battle-call of the conch-shell. It is difficult to tell who is your friend versus your foe. Your followers are flatterers, but they secretly take sides with your enemies.

Kans: [*thinking*] The rebel youth Krishna! A new order!
[*Pradyot enters and bows.*]

Pradyot: Glory be to the Royal God!

Kans: Is it true that the youth in Mathuraa are organizing a rebellion against my rule?

Pradyot: Yes, my God!

Kans: Is it also true that the flute is the symbol of this rebellion?

Pradyot: Yes, my God!

Kans: Then, is it also true that you are one of them?

Pradyot: No, my God!

Kans: [*screaming impatiently*] Then why didn't you send me this information in Magadh ?

Pradyot: I conveyed this information to the High Priest, Pralamb. It was his responsibility to send it to you in Magadh .

Kans: You are my childhood companion. You are my friend. I have confidence in you. But I no longer have faith in the Yaadav people. I place the responsibility of looking after the royal palace into the hands of the Magadh army chief, Vritrighn. You, Pradyot, shall also work under him.

Pradyot: As you wish, my Royal God.

Kans: Now you may leave.
[*Pradyot bows and exits.*]

Kans: What does Krishna look like?

Vritrighn: Dark, beautifully dark. Despite being dark,

he is very handsome.

Kans: Have it proclaimed that the first duty of every follower of Kans' religion is to punish those loose and lecherous young men and women who gather for music and love-making in the deserted parts of the forest.

Vritrighn: Your command shall be executed.
[*He bows and exits.*]
[*Kans stands in a reverie. Asti enters, limping, carrying a sandal in one hand.*]

Asti: I am in such pain, I can't even walk. I am talking to you, Kans! What the hell? Do you hear me?
[*Kans does not reply.*]
[*angrily*] Fine, if you won't listen, then don't! [*She goes away, limping angrily.*]
[*Kans stands, unmoved. Swaati appears in his mind's eye.*]

FLASHBACK WITHIN FLASHBACK BEGINS

Swaati: [*enters limping*] There's a thorn in my foot. [*She hops on one foot, while groaning.*] What are you staring at? Take it out!

Kans: [*taking her foot in his hand and looking at the sole*] Is the thorn here?

Swaati: Look closely. It's there somewhere.

Kans: I can't see it.

[*Swaati laughs. Kans looks at her wondrously. She continues laughing.*]

Kans: [*puzzled*] Why are you laughing?

Swaati: [*laughing*] There's no thorn, actually...

Kans: Then…

Swaati: [*victoriously*] I will now tell my friends that the Prince of Mathuraa has touched my feet.
[*Kans, in a huff, pushes her foot away. She runs away laughing. Kans, still lost in reverie, smiles.*]

Flashback within flashback ends

[*Asti enters, again limping.*]

Asti: Listen to me!
[*The smile leaves Kans' face.*]

Asti: What are you dreaming about? Please remove this thorn.

Kans: What happened?

Asti: His Lordship is asking what happened? After such a long time?...Were you in a trance?

Kans: What happened?

Asti: A thorn got into my foot. Please take it out.

Kans: Ask a maid…

Asti: If a maid could have done it, would I have asked you? It hurts a lot. Please do remove it.

Kans: [*looking at the sole of her foot*] Where is the thorn?

Asti: It's somewhere there.

Kans: I don't see it.

Asti: [*raising her skirt up to her knee*] Why don't you look more closely?
[*Kans roughly releases her foot. Asti laughs mischievously. Kans moves away and stands, motionless.*]

Asti: Is his Lordship annoyed? I was just joking.
[*Kans does not answer.*]

Asti: I came to show you this ruby necklace. My royal father sent it from Magadh .
[*Asti comes near Kans and, under the pretense of showing him the necklace, tries to draw his attention to her full, round breasts.*]

Asti: How do you like it?

Kans: [*indifferently*] It's very beautiful. [*He stands with his back towards the audience.*]

Asti: These shining stars against the backdrop of the dark sky, like innumerable diamonds in the black gown of night! Beautiful moonlight! The fragrance of flowers wafting in the cool breeze! The sky bending over the earth to take her in his embrace! [*to Kans*] Doesn't this cool breeze stimulate your veins with the exciting warmth of blood? Does the fair moonlight not raise a tide of restlessness in your heart? Doesn't the intoxicating night cause your body to sound like a flute...Don't your clothes feel too tight a trapping to stand? Don't you feel compelled to cast off your clothes to become one with this beauty? [*She leans against Kans' back.*] Doesn't the night whisper anything to you?

[*Kans moves away from Asti unceremoniously.*]

Kans: I don't have time for this nonsensical talk.

Asti: What's happened to you? What troubles your heart so much? [*moving closer*] Look at me. Look into my eyes. Does anyone else have such beautiful eyes? [*She opens her bun and spreads her hair over Kans' shoulder.*] Upon seeing the opulence of my hair, even the dark clouds will feel inferior to me. The scent of this body can make anyone feel faint. [*She places Kans' hand on her breast.*] Brimming with love...

[*Kans pulls his hand away.*]

My narrow waist, smooth thighs, my perfect figure! Is there any other in this whole world who possesses such incomparable beauty? Kans! Kans, what has happened to you? You can neither laugh nor cry like a normal person. [*She clings to him.*] Why can't you make love to me like any ordinary human being?

Kans: Because I am no longer an ordinary human being.

Asti: What are you now?

Kans: I am God. God *Shree* Kans!

Asti: Why are you God *Shree* Kans?

Kans: Because I am God. [*He roughly pushes her away; she falls to the ground.*]

Asti: [*vengefully*] I know why the God is so worried. Krishna, the leader of the Yaadav youths is organizing resistance against God *Shree* Kans' despotism! Innumerable young men and women support him. They hide in forests and caves, attack your soldiers, and then go back into hiding. [*Teasingly*] I hear that the youth leader Krishna is very handsome. He is dark, but his figure is so winsome that girls are all over him. I also want to see him once.

[*Kans glares at her angrily.*]

I want to see the one who steals the hearts of so many women! He must be so brave, to organize rebellion against God! Resistance against God *Shree* Kans! [*contemptuously*] God! The God who is impotent!

[*Kans spontaneously raises his hand to strike Asti, but refrains.*]

Kans: Your face is beautiful like the moon. Your lovely black eyes, your rose petal lips, proud high breasts, narrow waist and heavy thighs—I find them all repulsive. [*Kans suddenly grabs her by the throat and strangles her to death. He lowers her dead body to the ground, gazes at her for a minute, and then kisses her forehead.*]

[*in a choked voice*] You are free! Free, my love! Your soul, tender like the early morning dew, has been released to the eternity of the infinite sky. And I, Kans… [*almost crying*] your husband, your murderer...No, Asti, I have not murdered you. [*with conviction*] I have only murdered that counter-ego, which my ego could not present, be it of wife or friend, sister or father. That had to be destroyed. [*He sounds the gong three times.*]

[*The Guard enters.*]

Queen Asti went for a stroll in the garden. A snake bit her and she died. Take away her dead body. She shall be given a funeral with full State honors.

[*Lights fade out briefly, during which Asti exits from the stage.*]

Flashback xii ends

[*Pralamb enters.*]

Pralamb: The Royal God sent for me?

Kans: I want to ask you something.

Pralamb: I await your command.

Kans: Is Pralamb, the Archpriest of Kans' religion, a

friend or a foe?

Pralamb: What does the Royal God think?

Kans: Is it true that the flute-wielding Yaadav youths are organizing themselves to destroy my power?

Pralamb: Yes, my God.

Kans: And you never sent me news in Magadh ?

Pralamb: No, my God.

Kans: [*shouting*] Why not?

Pralamb: Because I am your enemy, wishing your destruction.

Kans: [*hurt*] Pralamb!

Pralamb: Since these are the last moments of my life, I will not lie.

Kans: Why did you do this?

Pralamb: Because I wanted to.

Kans: Why did you want to?

Pralamb: I am the illegitimate son of King Ugrasen, your father. My mother was never married to him. She was an orphan, a concubine of the King, who was so proud of his high birth and wealth that she offered the oblation of her body in worship of his lust. As a result, she got Pralamb! An illegitimate son, Pralamb! Ugly, hunchbacked Pralamb!

Kans: I know that.

Pralamb: You know nothing. I realized that I was the eldest son of King Ugrasen. I have the first claim to the Yaadav throne. I am your elder brother.

Kans: [*scornfully*] Elder brother…!

Pralamb: How could the illegitimate son of a lowly born mother become the Chief of the Yaadav Kingdom? There were two claimants, you and Vasudev. For me, both were the same. I made up my mind that whoever was made King would be the object of my revenge.

Kans: Ungrateful, sinful wretch! I will have you punished as an example to the rest of the world. You shall be tortured, bit by bit. Every part of your body will be pierced slowly. You will cry, yearn and beg for death, but you shall not be allowed to die.

Pralamb: I am not afraid of death or torture. I have known that this will be my fate for years. I have been waiting for it.

Kans: Today, I will end your waiting.

Pralamb: My aim was to raise you so high that when you fall crashing, you would not be able to bear it. I have succeeded in my mission. You are falling from those lofty heights today. All the Yaadav have turned against you. Your trusted followers are with the rebels.

[*Kans sounds the gong three times.*]
My dream has become a reality before my death. Today, I am the happiest man in the world. But Kans, today you are the unhappiest man. You are standing, terror-stricken, amidst the crumbling walls of the edifice you yourself have built—alone like a ghost, dead before death.
[*Two Hangmen enter. They escort Pralamb out after a signal from Kans.*]

Kans: You are so happy. You'll die happy. I envy you, Pralamb.
[*The notes of a flute are heard, at which Kans appears frightened.*]

Kans: Again the flute. Pradyot has still not succeeded in finding that cowherd boy Krishna.
[*Pradyot and the Guard enter. Both bow.*]

Pradyot: I have searched every nook and cranny of the palace. Krishna is not hiding here.

Kans: But that flute...?

Pradyot: How can Krishna enter the palace? Not even a bird can break through the security. Plus, security arrangement charges have been given to the Magadh soldiers, under Magadh Commander Vritrighn, whom you trust.

Kans: Do you object to this?

Pradyot: No, my God.

Kans: Now that the burden of safeguarding the palace

has been transferred from you to the Magadh Commander and soldiers, aren't you unhappy?

Pradyot: No, my God.

Kans: Then where could the flute be heard from?

Pradyot: From nowhere, my Royal God.

Kans: I heard it myself.

Pradyot: It's just your imagination.

Kans: Imagination, indeed! My army chief tells me that my mind is full of hallucinations!

Pradyot: [*afraid*] No, my Royal God.

Kans: I'm distracted! [*He moves forward to sound the gong.*]

Pradyot: [*in a commanding tone*] Wait, Kans.
[*Kans stops short of sounding the gong.*]

Pradyot: I want to ask you just one question.

Kans: Traitor!

Pradyot: [*challenging*] Who is the traitor? What treachery?

Kans: You are the traitor; the treachery is yours.

Pradyot: That's a lie.

Kans: It's the truth.
Pradyot: A lie.

Kans: In the face of your impending death…

Pradyot: I am not afraid of death. I want the answer to just one question.

Kans: Nonsense...

Pradyot: [*in a commanding tone*] You will have to answer me. [*He pauses a moment.*] Are you happy? [*Kans does not answer.*]

Pradyot: Why aren't you saying anything? I have served you all my life. I don't regret that. I don't know what infatuation caused me to do it. I have voluntarily carried out your every wish, just like a slave. But today, I see you clearly, in your true colors. Selfish, ugly, cruel and hateful... [*He spits on Kans, who wipes it off.*] I have served you of my own free will. I will also die of my own free will. [*He stabs himself with a dagger and dies.*]

Kans: One more killing. Is every death a suicide? The fearful eagles, circling high in the sky, the innocent eye of some child in the beak of a vulture, a lump of a woman's fair breast, dripping with blood, the sharp beak of a vulture, piercing the muscle of a strong youth's arm; women and children, young and old, all like lifeless puppets. Heaps upon heaps of innumerable corpses. Underneath them, buried deep—one corpse…The corpse of Kans. [*A flute is heard.*]

Kans: Again, the same flute. The flute communicating fear to every fibre of my being. [*suddenly, in a changed tone*] Am I terrified? No. I, the most powerful, the bravest, the brightest God *Shree* Kans, am not afraid of anything. My wish is supreme. My command is law. Whoever raises his head against me will be beheaded. Whoever frowns at me will have his eyes plucked out. I am invincible. I, the most powerful, the bravest, the brightest…

[*A flute is heard again.*]

There's the flute again!...That flute! [*He breaks down with fear.*] No…No… [*imploring*] No—no Krishna! No! [*as if begging for his life*] No, Krishna! No!

[*The flute fades out and the final music takes over, indicating the end.*]

CURTAIN

'THE KING OF MATHURAA ': Photographs from an earlier production in India

The Hindi plays written by the author

- Itihaas-Chakra
- Oh! America
- Katha Ek Kans Ki
- Apne-Apne Daon
- Saadar Apka
- Man Ke Bhanvar
- Rakt-Abhishek
- Samrat Ashok
- Dusman
- Itihaas
- Mere Bhai Mere Dost
- Seediyan
- Hasya Ekanki

The awards

- Akademi Award (the highest National Award for playwriting) by Sangeet Natak Akedemi, New Delhi
- Lohia Sahitya Samman by Uttar Pradesh Hindi Sansthan, Lucknow
- Sahitya Bhushan by Hindi Sansthan, Lucknow
- Bhuvaneshwer Samman by Bhuvaneshwar Shodh Sansthan, Shahjahanpur
- Akademi Puraskar by Uttar Pradesh Sangeet Natak Akademi, Lucknow
- Sanskriti Puraskar by Uttar Pradesh Government
- Sahityakar Samman by Delhi Hindi Akademi
- Urmila Mishra Smriti Award by Madhya Bharatiya Hindi Sahitya Sabha, Gwalior
- Bhavbhuti Samman by Natyaayan, Gwalior, Madhya Pradesh
- Fida Husain Narsee Award by Adarsh Kala Sangam, Moradabad, U.P.
- Chamanlal Memorial Award for lifetime achievement and contribution to theatre by Chamanlal Memorial Society, New Delhi
- NBC Newsmakers'Lifetime Achievement Award for Literature by NBC Newsmakers, Mumbai
- 'Lifetime Achievement Award for Hindi' by Hindi Vishwa Jyoti, California, USA